BY HAROLD BLOOM

SHELLEY'S MYTHMAKING

THE VISIONARY COMPANY
A Reading of English Romantic Poetry

BLAKE'S APOCALYPSE
A Study in Poetic Argument

Commentary to THE POETRY AND PROSE OF
    WILLIAM BLAKE (edited by D. V. Erdman)

YEATS

THE RINGERS IN THE TOWER
Studies in Romantic Tradition

THE ANXIETY OF INFLUENCE
A Theory of Poetry

A MAP OF MISREADING

KABBALAH AND CRITICISM

POETRY AND REPRESSION
Revisionism from Blake to Stevens

FIGURES OF CAPABLE IMAGINATION

WALLACE STEVENS
The Poems of Our Climate

THE FLIGHT TO LUCIFER

D1600346

The Flight to Lucifer

Harold Bloom

Farrar · Straus · Giroux 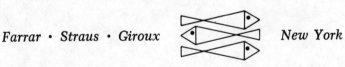 *New York*

The Flight to Lucifer

A GNOSTIC FANTASY

COPYRIGHT © 1979 BY HAROLD BLOOM
ALL RIGHTS RESERVED
PRINTED IN THE UNITED STATES OF AMERICA
PUBLISHED SIMULTANEOUSLY IN CANADA
BY MCGRAW-HILL RYERSON LTD., TORONTO
DESIGNED BY IRVING PERKINS
FIRST EDITION, 1979

LIBRARY OF CONGRESS CATALOGING IN PUBLICATION DATA
BLOOM, HAROLD.
THE FLIGHT TO LUCIFER.
I. TITLE.
PZ4.B65377F   1979   [PS3552.L6392]   813'.5'4   78-31897

For John Hollander

Contents

What makes us free is the Gnosis
    of who we were
    of what we have become
    of where we were
    of wherein we have been thrown
    of whereto we are hastening
    of what we are being freed
    of what birth really is
    of what rebirth really is

The Flight to Lucifer

CHAPTER 1

The Living Book of Olam

OLAM CAME down to Krag Island on an evening in late May. He came down from the spheres of the living Aeons, spheres as much superior to this world as any living person is superior to his or her image.

His descent was difficult. The Archons intervened against him several times. Knowing they could not stop Olam, they determined to hinder him. But what appeared to be the craft that transported him slipped through the storms that the world-making principalities raised against it. When it emerged from the gateway of a black hole, Olam woke up from a long sleep. For a few moments he did not know where he was, and his yellow eyes blinked uncertainly in the inner darkness out of which he stared. He had been dreaming the living book of his everlasting life as an Aeon, and in the moment of awakening he held that entire book together in a single mental image.

In the beginning was the Pleroma, the Fullness of thirty Aeons, who made up the Chariot that was also the Abyss, a Depth that was there first, before existence. Or rather (as Olam thought and saw it) the true Fullness—before even the beginning, before the Pleroma—was one perfect Aeon and with him his thought and sight, she who was his silence and his grace.

Yet from that beginning eventually had come the Kenoma, a cosmic emptiness into which all had been thrown. Olam peered out through a crystal transparency in his craft, coldly contemplating the infinite immensity of spaces which did not know him. What was it but a world of eyeless will, of mindless power? And what kept it in existence? Ignorance.

Olam's care in coming down was to seek again the true seer of the knowing called the Gnosis. Across space, from Alexandria to Point Rachel in New England, and eighteen centuries across time, he quested again for a prophet, the one who had been his companion in the old battles against the Archons.

"And who will not remember me, perhaps."

The sound of his own voice surprised him, as did his realization that he looked forward to seeing Valentinus again. Being an Aeon, Olam had known implicitly the meaning of his own history, but he had learned from the doctrine that made the meaning explicit; he had watched the doctrine of Valentinus vanish from most of this cosmos, while seeing also its survival in a few worlds not so afflicted by time as the earth was. Coming down closer to earth, he understood more clearly than before how dark its history was, and how much of the struggle remained his own.

Knowledge, the Gnosis, was spread out before him as he stared at the wide prison of space and contrasted it to the spheres of the Aeons. The Gnosis was *in* the contrast, in Olam's overwhelming realization that this cosmos of darkness around him, so apparently the spatial home of the human planet and its companions, was absolutely alien to mankind and to God. Neither man nor God had made, or ruled in, these terrible spaces, which had been created by the Archons and ever since had been mis-governed by them. This solar system, ruled by the Archon called Elohim, was as much a dungeon as any wretched stone cellar, with its inhabitants locked into earth by a cosmic warden. Laws of nature, instituted by the Archon, enslaved earth's universe and blocked even the ascent of the souls after death. The Creator or Demiurge, Ialdabaoth, miscalled Jehovah, had fashioned his entrapments most subtly.

The small blue globe of earth appeared before Olam. Whereas hitherto he had been traveling forward, now, in the region of gravity and its centrality, his flight became a descent. A great sadness moved him as he stared at the fragile world down to which as a messenger he had come before and now descended again in what would look, from the earth, like falling. The Fall was within the true Godhead and not among men, and the world's Fall was one with this beautiful ruin of a creation, which drew all who neared it down rather than up or into it.

At nine in the evening, Olam's craft brought him down gently onto the flat roof of a tower on Krag Island. He clambered down into the tower and walked through it. Though a hulking, hunched-over, yellow-complexioned figure, with a massive head all but sunk into its body, he moved with force and cunning always, shaking and disturbing even from here the spaces of the Archons.

CHAPTER **2**

Valentinus and Perscors

S E T H   V A L E N T I N U S got to bed a few minutes after nine that same night. He was accustomed to falling asleep just before dawn and to awakening after only two or three hours. But it had been an unusual day for him. Entering a room at ten that morning, he had stumbled and struck his head painfully on the door. A slight but persistent dizziness had caused him to cancel afternoon appointments. Medical examination had revealed nothing amiss, but the vertigo continued, and he sought relief by retiring at nine. Three dreams came to him before he woke at midnight.

In the first he voyaged upward and outward through a starry realm. The spacecraft seemed familiar to him, and yet a dread of something hovered nearby. "They will not

7

let me through," he heard himself saying. In his distress, he wandered through the ship and somehow emerged beyond it, floating by himself through the starry darkness. Intense pleasure attended his drifting, but the freedom which it reflected ceased when he came down upon a broad flat surface. He stood, a solitary mind among the waste places, hemmed in by endless emptiness.

The Archon stood before him, uttering repeatedly the one name: Ialdabaoth. Valentinus studied the eyes of the Archon. They were of all colors, but a blank white at the center. Then he realized that the Archon was blind.

Without willing himself to speak, Valentinus found himself denouncing the Archon: "Blind god and god of the blind! I am a word of the unmixed Spirit, a perfect work to the Father, bearing a symbol imprinted with the character of Life—I open the world-gate which you have locked, and I pass by, scorning your power. For I am free again."

But the Archon's huge face grew enormous and surrounded Valentinus, the sight of it pressing against him from all sides. The blank centers of the Archon's eyes became an ocean of whiteness, and in that ocean Valentinus bobbed along, desperately struggling not to drown.

The struggle yielded to waking and then to a second dream. A tower rose beside the sea. Valentinus descended from his flight to stand upon the tower's flat roof, where an ugly, yellow-eyed man stood before him, grinning cheerfully and benignly.

"Not know me, old companion? Come to me with your friend Perscors at midnight two days hence. Come to the tower in Bodman's Gully on Krag Island . . ."

Olam vanished, and Valentinus stood alone upon the

tower. A great wind blew in from the sea. Valentinus listened to the wind, and a menacing voice was in it:

"Heresiarch, be warned against returning to old ways. Beware of the demon Olam, lest he lead you to accursed worlds. The flight to Lucifer is an impiety . . ."

Valentinus leaned over the edge of the tower and fell forward, but without fear, and found himself in some kind of unimpelled flight over the sea. But storm clouds intervened, and he came down below them and finally stood on a small island. Out to sea was a line of rocks, each the size of a man, with the horizon seemingly just beyond them. Olam, not looking at Valentinus, was leaping from rock to rock; he then faded into the horizon. The rocks remained but seemed now more men than rocks, steadily moving in toward Valentinus. He focused upon the single one closest to him and saw a version of himself coming near. This other Valentinus cried out to him, but a wind carried the sound away, except for what seemed the single word: "Remember." As one Valentinus merged with another, the second dream dissolved into a third.

He sat in his office, facing a couch upon which lay his friend Thomas Perscors. Perscors faced away from Valentinus and talked in a steady drone; not one word was intelligible. Some other presence was in the room; it was invisible but its murmur could just be heard beyond the level of Perscors's voice. Another sound, a dull thud, came intermittently from the door.

The alien murmur grew until Valentinus could hear it as a voice. Its clarity of speech increased until he could make out its words:

". . . Since through 'Ignorance' came about 'Deficiency'

and 'Passion,' therefore the whole system springing from the Ignorance is dissolved by Knowledge . . ."

The voice fell away. Attempting to hold together and understand its statement, Valentinus felt a shock of memory, for it had been his own voice, and he had read or heard the formulation before. The murmur was gone, but the thuds at the door still punctuated Perscors's accompanying drone. A particularly hollow thud woke Valentinus, who cried out in pain. He listened for a moment, but with waking consciousness had come a deep silence. His watch showed midnight.

Pondering the three dreams confirmed his need to speak to Perscors. He knew his friend to be as sleepless as himself, and telephoned him. The two arranged to meet day after next in Point Rachel, so as to take the ferry to Krag Island. Valentinus had time enough to brood on "Deficiency," which more than "Passion" seemed his predicament and Perscors's as well. But he brooded even more on forgetfulness and wondered if that were his form of the "Ignorance."

He did not know how little he himself had changed, inwardly or outwardly, across the eighteen centuries in which he had lived and died in his incarnations, since his first existence in Alexandria. Dark, almost hairless, his body slender but tempered to every ordeal, he rarely looked other than grim and puzzled. An endless spiritual hunger conflicted in him with the failure of memory, though he knew that he had died from many previous lives, and that the first of them had been the most crucial.

Perscors knew nothing certain of his friend's experience of earlier incarnations. A giant of a man, good-natured but easily provoked to violence, he too had his version of a quester's temperament. A desire for the transcendental and extraordinary had led him to a series of debacles. What drew him to Valentinus was the obscure recognition that his friend finally would serve as a link to a spiritual apotheosis, to a crisis in which Perscors himself would be transformed or destroyed.

He did not know where or what Lucifer was, or why the voyage there was necessary. It would not have stopped him had he known that one of his traveling companions was an Aeon, a heretical angel by the canons of the faith in which Perscors had been raised. Nor would his departure have been prevented had he confirmed what he suspected, which was that his other companion, Valentinus, had indeed been reincarnated from earlier lives. The image of an inner fire, which had haunted him from childhood, flared more strongly than ever after his summons by Valentinus.

CHAPTER 3

On Krag Island

TWO AFTERNOONS later, Perscors and Valentinus took the Point Rachel ferry for Krag Island. The weather had changed suddenly that morning, with violent gusts and occasional fierce rain coming in from the coast. In the sharp chill of the ferry's upper deck, Perscors and Valentinus sat alone. The passengers who had not canceled their trip were all below, unwilling to confront the unusually cold air. Perscors gazed out over the sea swell, taking a savage satisfaction in the roughness and the dark sky, and wondering what was motivating his allegiance to this quest. Valentinus had volunteered little information, and Perscors therefore asked for nothing. He fought off the cold with a brandy flask, as the ferry heaved on, and he brooded on the insane notion that in only a few hours he would be on a flight to an unknown world.

A little after five, with evening coming on prematurely, Perscors and Valentinus left the ferry and walked off the dock onto Krag Island.

"How far have we to walk, Valentinus?"

"Bodman's Gully is less than two miles, Perscors, and so half an hour will do it. But there will be time enough to meet Olam. He is not likely to be early. I want to take you somewhere else, first."

"You know this island well, then? You have voyaged out beyond space from here before?"

Valentinus frowned, with a painful look of perplexity. "I don't know . . . I can't remember . . . Don't ask me to explain, but just come!"

The two friends set out on a path leading from the harbor to nearby sea cliffs. Each had only a light pack, and both were agile, determined climbers. Soon after reaching the cliffs, they began a rapid ascent, and within half an hour they stood together in a high spot, surrounded by whirling hawks whose nesting place had been disturbed.

"What have you brought me to see, Valentinus? The view is only another sight of ocean."

"I have brought you to *hear* something, not to *see*, Perscors. From this cliff you can hear very turbid water, water of the abyss, perhaps."

Both men stood quietly for a few moments. Perscors smiled and gestured at the hawks. "I can hear *them*, and the normal sounds of the sea, but nothing remarkable at all."

"No, I mean nothing *remarkable*," Valentinus commented. "Listen, listen very carefully, and see if you cannot hear something *alien* calling out to you."

Perscors shut his eyes and waited; after a few moments he could hear nothing, no wind or rain, no sound of waves, no bird cries. He listened intently to silence, and then he ceased to listen. A bewilderment came over him, then a fear, and finally a shock, as though an inward wind had begun to blow against him. From a great way off, faintly, he began to hear a call of waters, but a call that seemed to be *voiced*, as though a more primal ocean had been able to form speech. He began to hear it as a woman's voice calling out a name in a tone of desperate frenzy, and he responded with a terrifying sexual arousal. Straining to hear the name, he lost consciousness. A few moments later he found himself stretched out on the rocky ground, with Valentinus, worried, kneeling by him.

"What did you hear?" Valentinus demanded.

To his own amazement, Perscors found himself whispering a name unknown to him.

"Have you ever heard the name 'Achamoth,' or one like it?" he asked Valentinus, as he pulled himself to his feet.

"Yes, somewhere, once," Valentinus replied, standing up. "It means something like 'a woman's dark intention,' in some old tongue, but I do not think that was the alien call I expected you to hear. Though *what* I expected I still cannot remember clearly."

Perscors, a touch irritated both with himself and his friend, stared at him uneasily for a moment.

"You have a queer memory, Valentinus. You almost remember a great many mysteries, but when you come close up to them, something fails you."

Valentinus remarked only that it was growing dark, and he led the way down the sea cliff. After a walk on the twilit roads, which were nearly deserted, the two friends started down off the main way onto a footpath leading into Bodman's Gully. This was a large marshy stretch of ground marked by underwater vegetation, as the hollow was well below sea level. Valentinus led Perscors ever deeper into it, where the opulent vegetation began to assume a luxuriance that seemed more appropriate to another latitude. Soon there was no path, and Perscors was wondering what house could be located in so uncleared a place when suddenly he found himself standing in front of a round turret, apparently quite windowless, squat-looking yet towering up a surprising seventy feet to a curiously flat roof. Perscors reflected that this brown stone structure seemed at once banal in its ugly commonplaceness and sinister in its uncanny uniqueness.

CHAPTER 4

The Tower

THE TOWER, as Perscors now saw, was not only windowless but evidently without a door. In the cold, dim light he could make out no entrances as he walked about the tower, which seemed nearly as broad as it was tall. Perscors came back to where he had started his circuit, to find that Valentinus was digging vigorously at a spot a few yards in front of the tower. A tunnel was thus uncovered, through which Valentinus preceded Perscors, each of them employing a kerosene torch. The way was surprisingly long, longer than seemed reasonable to Perscors. Finally, Valentinus pulled himself up through a trapdoor. Perscors followed to the bare stone of the tower's first floor. The round room, as he probed it with his light, appeared to be totally empty except for the

circular steps leading up to the next floor, which seemed
to be lit up. Valentinus hesitated at the foot of the stairs.

"What is it?" Perscors asked impatiently. "There's
nothing on this level, is there?"

Before Valentinus could make any reply, Perscors was
startled by a whisper which did not seem to come from
any particular direction, A male voice, with a kind of
bitter or ironic sympathy, said to him: "Try to understand that Olam lied. There is no return from this flight,
not by the living. And Olam and Valentinus are not
among the living . . ."

The voice trailed off, even as Valentinus muttered:
"There is a presence here," but nonetheless, he started
up the stone stairs. Perscors followed, to find another
bare room; this one was brightly illuminated—how he
could not tell—from its walls.

"This room is empty also, Valentinus. Will the whole
tower be empty?"

"No, not so very empty," Valentinus answered, in a
soft, dry tone, as he stared at the walls. Projections had
come upon all the walls at once, as though cast upon
screens. But the images came and went so quickly that
Perscors, turning from wall to wall, could hardly follow
what might have been a sequence or story. As figure
merged into figure, actions seemed followed not by their
effects but by their causes. In the midst of this phantasmagoria he began to make out certain elements. A
Primal Man—naked, calm, majestic, godlike—appeared
walking upon a rocky shore, against the background
of an ocean without waves, a sky without color, blue sea
against white horizon. The man's face moved Perscors,
first to wonder, then to reverence, but finally to appre-
hension concerning the man himself, for it came to seem

that there was a bewilderment, not in the man's countenance, but in the random patterns of his walking.

This bewilderment was linked to another image. In
heights more suggested than seen, the man reclined
amid vistas hinting at an abyss of perfection, a formless-
ness more orderly than any form could be. As Perscors
watched, the man's face grew in size until it was one
with the serene abyss. Across this double vision of the
wandering and resting man a shadow fell, but a shadow
that seemed itself to be a grace. Suddenly the light grew
too brilliant upon that wall, and Perscors spun about to
the wall behind him. There the shadow fell large, and
confronting it, Perscors was overcome by desire, for the
shadow's grace was now a woman, whose dark, full face
expressed a great silence, a silence Perscors yearned to
enter. But this phantasmal gleam vanished also, and now
all the walls were blank with a fierce, numbing light.

Valentinus climbed to the tower's third level, which
was roughly furnished and lit in a more subdued way by
a single lantern upon each wall. Perscors, clambering up
after, asked no questions but looked about him with
curiosity at an oaken table, some chairs, a few cup-
boards, and one low couch set against a wall.

"Is this Olam's den?" he asked, but asked more of himself than as expecting any reply.

"We can't get farther up by ourselves," Valentinus
muttered, "so we must wait here for him, anyway. It is
almost five hours until departure, and he comes neither
early nor late. I am going to sleep."

Disdaining the couch, Valentinus curled up on the
floor and was asleep in a moment. Perscors felt anger
rising, and headed for the stairs to the fourth level. The
first touch of his foot on the first stair stunned him al-

most into unconsciousness. Only the terrible strength of his will kept him upright, for a force had flung him across the tower and against a wall. Though nearly overcome, he staggered toward the stairs again, furiously determined to mount them. His advance carried him up against a series of shocks, each sickening but none the equal of the original in impact. Confronting what seemed crystal walls on all sides, open translucently to the night sky, he stared in disbelief at radiances more burning than ever he had beheld, and then rested his eyes by looking about the room. There was one object only, a moving model of the cosmos, half as high as a man and occupying the room's center. Intricately carved, its metallic design gave off a loathsome aura, as though the artificer had done his work in overt horror of what he had so superbly imitated. The model seemed to be proclaiming the evil of what was represented, a proclamation conveyed by the sinister light, green-blue, in which the structure whirled about.

Perscors, fascinated and repelled, glanced down at the stone floor between him and the cosmic model. A single word glowed in the stone, in large irregular red letters, spelling out: HEIMARMENE. He did not know the word. Repeating it to himself, softly, he felt intensely ambivalent. He sensed that the word involved his destiny, and at once he welcomed it and rebelled against it. A voice, this time off to his right, spoke in the deep, full whisper of a woman: "Climb the stairs to the top, Perscors, and then leave your companions. Realize that this journey is intended *against* the star world, and against your heimarmene . . ."

The voice reverberated in his ear with a sensation itself passionate. Impatiently he shook it from him, but turned to mount the stairs to the fifth level, convinced that such had been his intention anyway. This time the stairs offered no resistance. He bounded up to an almost dark room, illumined fitfully as if by flares, yet with no sign of such agency. In the room's center was a single lectern, six feet high, with a slim parchment manuscript upon it. The vellum outer wrapper was stamped in gold: THE GOSPEL OF TRUTH. Perscors, turbulent with wonder, took up the manuscript and opened it, to find that most of its pages had been obliterated, torn or burned away, or else ruined by long exposure to watery air. But on the third page he could make out: "This Ignorance concerning the Father produced Anguish and Terror. And the Anguish became dense like a fog so that no one could see . . ." Some pages further on he was able to read: "It was a great marvel that they were in the Father without knowing Him . . ." Near the close, after many ruined pages, he found one consecutive passage:

"As a person's ignorance, at the moment when he comes to know, disintegrates of its own will; as darkness disintegrates when light appears; so also Deficiency dissolves with the advent of the Fullness. Surely thenceforward Shape is no longer apparent but will be extinguished in fusion with Unity, at the moment when Unity shall perfect the Aeons. So also shall each one of us receive himself back. Through knowledge he shall purge himself, by consuming the matter within himself like darkness to a dying flame . . ."

As he read this passage, Perscors heard a call to arms he felt he had heard before, where and when he could not recall. Despite his reverence for the words he had read, he knew that he understood them only in small part. If the flight to Lucifer, or anywhere else, could purge him to understanding, then he felt more than ready to depart; in this spirit he prepared himself to ascend to the tower's total darkness, and he was not surprised when his kerosene torch failed him as he mounted the stairs. He continued to climb up, but found himself almost breathless as he reached the final step. He dragged himself into the sixth room, and then he fainted. After a few moments, he recovered consciousness to find himself lying in darkness upon the icy-cold stone floor. Summoning all his powerful will, he rose to his knees. At once fire flamed about him. It seemed as if the tower's seventh and topmost floor had been burned away. An unbearable wave of heat flowed toward him. As Perscors lost consciousness again, his mind was noting that this agony of flame could not consume him, or even daunt him, but he fell into a heavy sleep even as he tasted his own pride.

CHAPTER **5**

Heimarmene

''H E I S a heavy sleeper, your giant," Olam grinningly remarked to Valentinus, who stared gloomily at the just-awakened Perscors, more than four hours later. Perscors was still lying on the stone floor of the sixth room, but now without sensations of heat or cold. The room was lit brightly from or through the walls, and the trapdoor to the tower's roof was open, at the top of a final circle of stairs. Lying on his back, Perscors looked up through the aperture into a starry sky,

"You have woken from your slumber," Olam said to Perscors, and added roughly: "But will you stay awake? You hear all sorts of calls, but will you ever tell one from another? Will your pleasure voyage turn into something more?" With his stranger's face yellow and jeering under

22

a broad-brimmed hat, Olam seemed ugly and formidable to Perscors. Angry at this provocation, Perscors felt his strength returning rapidly and rose to his feet.

"You are an odd host, Olam. Mythological films, two kinds of voices, models of the star world, ruined scriptures, fire and cold. Something to eat before departure, and a few explanations from you and Valentinus, would be more useful."

Valentinus maintained his usual silence, but Olam roared in amusement.

"You're in the great line, giant! You'll keep blundering on and perhaps break even *your* head on a truth before you end! Food's no problem. You'll eat now before we leave. But you won't understand, not at the point you've reached. Fire questers almost never come to *know*."

"Why take me along, then?" Perscors questioned. "If Valentinus *knows*, even if he can't remember much, what shall I be good for?"

"You come together," Olam said more quietly. "The quest needs you both, your soul and his spark. Where we are going, the combat is simpler than here, but just as bloody and twice as vital."

"Combat with whom or what, Olam?"

"You know the text," Olam answered, "though St. Paul got it backward, just exactly backward. *Our* strife really will be not against flesh and blood but against principalities, against the powers, against the world rulers of this present Darkness, and against the spiritual hosts of wickedness in the heavenly places. But we don't know yet, nor do you, whether *your* soul isn't part of those spiritual hosts."

Olam's full statement had been puzzling. Perscors stood in doubt, looking from this alien presence to Valentinus, waiting for his friend to speak. After a hesitation, Valentinus spoke harshly, addressing himself to Olam: "As we have got to go together, all of us, it is not a time to taunt each other with mysteries. *There* we will at least have a chance of knowing who and where we are."

"But *whom* are we going against?" Perscors burst out.

"Against the star world," Olam answered, "and in your case, perhaps against yourself. But we aren't the first, nor will we be the last, to set ourselves against the cosmos."

"You speak as though you were no part of the cosmos, Olam. What are you, anyway?"

But for once Valentinus started to speak of his own will, interrupting the others: "There isn't a way of explaining these things here, not on our world. So many times I've had to learn that. Risk everything, as I know you to be capable of doing, and then both of us will see more clearly."

After this appeal, Perscors was content. Olam led them back to the tower's third level, where they shared a meal of bread and brandy. They ate silently, as midnight came near. When they finished, Perscors turned to Olam: "Just one last question, anyway. What does heimarmene signify?"

"It means fate, oppressive cosmic fate. It pretends to be the law of the universe. The Babylonians invented it, and astrologists have played with it ever since. But the Greeks, and the best of them at that, made it a philosophic religion. Pythagoras called it a harmony, and he invented the psyche, your precious soul, as an effluence from it, so that part of your mind would be an overflow from the stars. But you have a spirit also, your pneuma, a kind of spark, that isn't your soul and that is older and better than the stars. We are going so as to give you a chance to purge yourself of your soul, and to let that spark blaze up again into the light beyond the stars."

For some moments, all three sat in silence. Perscors had more to absorb than the abundance that already had flooded him. Resolving to brood upon all this later, he confined himself to one pragmatic question: "I am ready to leave, with a whole heart. What is the ship?"

Olam proudly replied: "I cross the cosmos through black holes. Even if a craft came close to the speed of light, it would not be fast enough, for these light-years are beyond your span. The escape from heimarmene is through the black holes. In their density, their gravity is so strong that everything is pulled into them. All of light comes in, including every spark of spirit."

"But how do we enter a black hole so as to come out of it again? Where do you find your gateway or window?"

"That is part of the knowing" was all that Olam would answer.

"What, then, is the spacecraft?"

Olam laughed with the weariness of too many questions.

"An illegal borrowing, from your space shuttle perhaps. We will say no more about that. Instead, we will depart, now! No space suits or helmets required, either for how we go or where we go. You'll breathe an ordinary sea-level atmosphere of nitrogen and oxygen, on the flight and on Lucifer."

He stood and led the way up the tower, Valentinus following him, and Perscors, heart pounding, coming after. This time the fourth level offered no obstacles. On the tower's flat roof, the spacecraft waited, and they entered.

"I am the pilot," Olam said as Perscors glanced about him. "We will be a while on this crossing, and by the nature of it you will have to sleep. But it will be a good sleep, a dreamless sleep, almost like a good death."

Perscors did not bother to react. His heart was set on Lucifer, and his weariness with Olam seemed now as intense as his weariness with the earth he was leaving. He turned and, as though sleepwalking, went to the nearest bunk and sank into it. In a moment he was in profound sleep.

Valentinus walked over to the bunk and studied the features of his sleeping friend. "Will I see him again, Olam?"

"How can I say, Valentinus? I only know what we must do when we get there. What *will* happen, I cannot know. But this one seems subtler than the others, as well as stronger. There may be enough of the spark in him. He will have his chance."

Valentinus turned away, to his own meditations. Olam went to the controls, and within moments the flight to . Lucifer had begun.

CHAPTER **6**

The Mandaeans

W H E N H E awoke, Perscors found himself lying by the bank of a wide river in a green valley. Years before, he had been in Iraq and had walked along the lower Euphrates. As he began to walk by this river, he wondered if he were back at the Euphrates, so reminiscent was the landscape. Then he stopped and looked about him. Olam, Valentinus, and the spacecraft were gone, and he was alone on a planet far away from earth, on the other side of the cosmos. He felt neither terror nor wonder.

Looking to his right, away from the river, he saw that he was not alone. A tall, gaunt man, but not so tall as himself, walked toward him across a meadow. The man, dressed in what seemed an aristocratic version of a shepherd's smock, carried a large shepherd's crook, which to Perscors seemed as much a weapon as a badge of office. Perscors silently waited to be welcomed.

"In the name of the great first alien Life from the worlds of light, the sublime that stands above all works, I greet you." The man announced himself as Enosh, leader of the Mandaeans, and demanded knowledge of Perscors's identity, origins, and purposes.

"Perscors. I come from afar, across the black holes of space, and I believe I seek no enemy."

Enosh studied him closely, and then smiled.

"You have come to the wrong world, then, for here you must choose a side."

"Is there no peace on a world named the light-bearer?"

"We are surrounded by the Sethians" was the unsmiling reply. "And *they* have enemies to both sides of them, and so it goes, on to their enemies' enemies, and ever so on to the end of this world. We are all exiled from Light and Life together, but some have the knowledge of the exile, while most do not. And those who do not know war incessantly against the Knowers."

"I have no clear understanding of what I know or do not know. I came here with a stranger, named Olam, and with my friend Valentinus, but they would seem to have flown off again without me."

Enosh thought for a few moments. "If Olam brought you, it must have been for some good purpose. Of Valentinus I have no acquaintance. Where do you mean to go, once you have breakfasted among our tents?"

Perscors turned around and pointed to the river.

"An impulse tells me that I am to cross this river and go westward."

"We can land you on the other bank," said Enosh reluctantly, "but no one will go with you. And whether the Sethians will harm you, I cannot say. But come now, and eat with us."

He led Perscors across the meadow, into some low hills, until they entered the armed camp of the Mandaeans. Perscors, looking around him at the many curious but not friendly faces, saw a shepherds' community of some seven hundred, a spare, gaunt, rugged-looking people. The men were armed with lances, swords, bows, and the formidable pastoral crooks. The Mandaeans ate at long communal tables, gathered together as families, except for Enosh and Perscors, who sat together to eat under a tree. An armed retainer served them goat's milk, cheese, and bread. They ate in silence, as Perscors studied a pale-blue sky, lit by a sun that seemed smaller and less luminous than the sun he had known on earth.

"What is the quarrel between you and the Sethians? Is it actually a religious matter?"

Enosh hesitated for a long interval, and then spoke with great bitterness: "At root, it is religious, but on the surface it is the common quarrel about possession of land. If you cross west over the river, somewhat farther down from here, you come to haunted ground. Ages ago, it was holy, for we and the Sethians agree that the Pleroma was there. Now it is only a legacy, useful for grazing, and for dreaming. But we claim it, they dispute our claim, and we and they raid one another's flocks there."

"How far down the river is it?" Perscors asked.

"About an hour's march. Do you mean to go there first?"

Perscors found he could not answer, as images began to flood his mind. He recognized some of them as being from the projections of a particular man and landscape on the walls of the tower on Krag Island, and felt a connection to the place which Enosh had called the Pleroma.

"What was the Pleroma?"

"It was the world of Perfection, of the Fullness of thirty Aeons, in fifteen harmonious pairs. There, in the great heights (for which we have no name) dwelled the Abyss, our Forefather."

"It is a strange thing, to call an Abyss your god," said Perscors. "The religions I know oppose God the Father to the Abyss. He broods on the Abyss and creates out of it."

"They are lies, those religions." Enosh spoke with flat, cold emphasis. A silence ensued.

"Will you not tell me more of the Pleroma, Enosh?"

"No; as you are going to its place, its ghostly voices can tell you, if they choose, and if you live to get there."

Another silence followed, making it clear to Perscors that it was time to leave the Mandaeans. Enosh seemed to him a fanatic who could neither teach nor learn. By noon, Perscors had been ferried across the nameless river. He had discovered among his increasingly reluctant hosts a great fear of naming, and he felt relief at being abandoned by the Mandaeans on the Sethian bank of the river. The Sethians, he reflected, could be no worse than this fearful, narrow, aggressive remnant of a people that he had left behind him.

For about an hour, he walked down the path. Even at midday, the sun beaming down upon Lucifer seemed rather grudging in its heat, and the damp chill increased as he walked. Gradually he became aware that the meadows were changing. The foliage grew so dark in its green as to appear almost black. A miasma hung over the land, and thickened on the riverbank. Vigorous as he was, Perscors began to weary. Surely he had marched for more than an hour, and except for the rankness increasing about him, no particular place, haunted or not, came to view.

He glanced at the river and realized that it had changed, being now more a sluggish marsh than a river. After another space, he came to see that there was no longer a path, and so he stopped, caked in mud to the knees. Looking up again, he saw a woman watching him. She stood a few yards away, half concealed in her nakedness by the rushes, and laughed at him mischievously. Despite exhaustion and surprise, he was charmed instantly and wholly. The exhaustion left him as he moved toward her. Still smiling, she retreated into the rushes and was gone, and he failed to find her, as he went deeper and deeper into the rushes, away from the river. Something in her face had intoxicated him, and he felt no other memory, no other desire than the need to see that face again.

Some moments later, as he plunged on, Perscors was astonished to find that he was climbing and that the ground under him was now rock. Without apparent transition, he was in another region, with awesome heights ahead of him. As he toiled upward, visions of her face continued to torment him. However briefly glimpsed, the face had joined itself to the daydreams he could recall even from his boyhood, intimations of a grace and glory that no woman since had fulfilled.

A different sense of dream now began to possess him, as the heights rose at angles so sharp that he was compelled to stop climbing. His dilemma was now insoluble

—he could go no farther, yet could not turn back. He was exposed on what had become a veritable precipice, and without aid could make no further efforts. The necessities of survival drove from him his memory of the woman.

"An absurd end," he rasped, and his spirit urged him upward. He attacked the heights above him in a fierce rush, and against his own sense of preposterousness at the angle of ascent, he achieved a further stance at a less exposed place. Though he could not get back, it now seemed as if he might climb forward; yet he sensed that he was climbing into a kind of abyss. An intense cold, which he could not bear, surrounded him. In a last effort of desperation, he threw himself onward again, gained the heights, and stood erect on a vast tableland, empty and austere. And in a moment he realized, rather than saw, that he had reached the place of the Pleroma.

CHAPTER 7

Caves of Ruha

B Y P E R S C O R S ' S reckoning, it should have been no more than early afternoon, yet he stood on the tableland in twilight. Though the bitter cold had abated, a strong wind blew against him. In the uncertain light, he sensed that there were presences in front of him, but still at considerable distances away. The will to go forward, whether to or against them, was strong in him, yet he felt his solitude in a way he never had experienced. He examined, as best he could in the growing darkness, the scene before him.

No part of Enosh's description seemed true, since this huge, rocky plain hardly could be disputed as grazing land. But Perscors had learned already, in his few hours on the planet, that both time and place were curiously

33

inconstant on Lucifer. He had learned also to trust his own daemonic inwardness, which told him now that he stood upon enchanted ground, and which encouraged him to explore the mysteries that awaited him. His earthly sense of failure had left him, whether in the tower or on Lucifer he could not tell, and in its stead had come a keen sense of election. On this world, where lost eras of earth's spiritual history seemed to linger, he had found in himself a conviction of purposiveness. So far, it was a purposiveness without purpose, but he felt that the meaning would be revealed, and would be a true test for him. His ignorance might be a dark fire, but it was a fire nevertheless, and he believed he would burn through every concealment that Lucifer might thrust between his spark and the truth.

He began to walk toward what he took to be the center of the plateau. The ground was more uneven than he had expected, and his way was slow. Darkness came on. He looked upward and studied a clear, starry sky totally unfamiliar to him, and toward which he felt neither affection nor hostility. Remembering suddenly some reference to Lucifer as "a moony world," he decided that moonrise came later and was grateful for the amount of starlight he could see.

A few moments farther on, he had to stop, because the uneven ground was giving way to small hills and to unexpected gullies. Climbing out of a sudden declivity, he confronted what might have been the entrance to a cavern in a hillside and followed his impulse by going up to it. It seemed dark and uninhabited, but the strange thought came that *he* would illumine it. He went in, lowering his head, and after a few feet turned sharply to his right. Several steps ahead, a light glimmered at another such turning. Rounding this, he approached the bright entrance to a cave-within-a-cave. He went through, and confronted the woman he had seen so briefly at the river.

She was clothed now in a green robe, and stood waiting for him. The uncanny conviction that she was not mortal came as a warning to him, but he refused the presage. On this world, where all else was inconstant, he knowingly had been thrown into a permanent desire, and he felt no will to resist this aspect of his heimarmene. But though he followed her freely, as she turned and led him more deeply into what became a labyrinth, he was conscious of a detachment in some residue of his being. He thought back to Olam's distinction between Valentinus and himself, and wondered if it was his psyche or soul that followed the woman, while his pneuma or spark stood apart.

These thoughts receded as he marveled at the intricacies of the labyrinth through which he trailed the form of his desire. An underground river appeared, some six turns in, directly after they had passed through an arch shaped like the mouth of a sea beast. The noise of the river increased as they walked, a noise for which Perscors was grateful, as it worked against a sleepiness that was intensifying within him. Such drowsiness he attributed to the change in the caverns, which had become gardens, lit by a green-black light that seemed to emanate from below. Obscurely, Perscors half remembered lines from an old poem about such gardens, at once "goodly garnishèd/With herbs and fruits" but also "direfull deadly blacke both leafe and bloom."

They came at last to what seemed a midpoint in the gardens. In a shaded arbor, the woman lay down upon a silver divan. Perscors hesitated and then joined her. Confusedly, he lost any sense of dream, since knowing her body brought back a fuller sense of reality; yet the exuberance of his sexual response immediately became a kind of drunkenness. Except for whispering "Ruha" in response to his demand for her name, she made love silently and with no change in her half-mocking expression. How many times Perscors entered her, he could not tell. Except for the terrible intensity of his comings, and a baffled sense of desire continually provoked rather than fulfilled, the embraces at first differed little from those he had experienced in his life on earth. But they began to change. Even as the sense of drunkenness started to weaken Perscors, a series of painful jolts went through his body and rendered him unconscious.

When he recovered, he was alone. Ruha's torn robe and his own disarray were what remained of his first union on Lucifer. He washed himself at the river, and yielded to acute hunger, eating some yellow apples, bitter but disintoxicating. Bewilderment followed. Had she gone farther into the caverns, or had she turned back to the hollow hill on the tableland of the Pleroma? His questing temperament directed Perscors onward. But the labyrinthine turns soon branched out so many ways, all somehow accompanied by the river, that he determined to go back to the arbor if he could. His wanderings continued, for some hours as it seemed to him, until he realized that his movement was circular. Weariness overwhelmed him. He lay down in a cypress grove on the riverbank and brooded on the riddle of the woman until he slept.

CHAPTER **8**

The Sethians

PERSCORS WOKE to his second morning on Lucifer. His dreams had been of the woman—of her straight-
combed, long, black hair, parted in the middle; of her
black eyes detachedly contemplating him; of the red
bow of her mouth suddenly transformed into an arch
that became the mouth of a sea monster. He had been
thrown into that mouth, to find himself reposing at sea
bottom. In a coral-walled sphere, he had lain helpless
while watching pages drift by him, pages torn from a
scripture he needed to have read. Sometimes a page
sailed near enough for him to read some phrases, and
these lingered in him now as he brushed river water into
his eyes.

"Ruha and the stars forged plans . . . They took the

living water and poured turbid water into it . . . the mystery of drunkenness . . . They took the head of the tribe and practiced on him the mystery of love and of lust, through which all the worlds are inflamed. They practiced on him seduction, by which all the worlds are seduced."

He could make out little meaning in these fragments, nor could he remember having read them anywhere. His resolution, as he left the cypress grove, was to break out of the labyrinth, and his usual confidence had come back to him. But he was unable to judge among directions, and much walking merely began to numb him, as the gardens and the river showed only small variation. Rounding one turn with particular haste and anger, he was thrown precipitately from a considerable height into what seemed a tidal marsh.

Stunned, he scrambled out of the bog and lay exhausted and filthy on a red clay surface. Above him were the heights from which he had been thrown. His clay refuge was an island in a panorama of marshes, leading to the river that separated the Mandaeans and Sethians.

As Perscors recovered some strength, he vowed to himself that he had been thrown for the last time. No shocks or fires, sudden falls or ecstasies of embrace were to overcome him again! Very carefully, he made his way to the Euphrates-like river, where he washed himself. His clothes were now sodden rags, and he was very hungry, but the dim morning sun was warm enough. He turned to the question of aim: ought he now to go west, perhaps to catch up with Olam and Valentinus, or was he to find again the place of the Pleroma, whether to learn its mysteries or to hold Ruha again and question her?

In the midst of his meditation, he sensed danger and moved back from the river to conceal himself in the rushes. Armed men appeared on both sides of the river. A band of twenty archers, whom he took to be Sethians, were a few yards from him, opposing about the same number of Mandaeans on the other bank. Each force shot against the other, but all the arrows simply fell in the river. As neither band had boats, Perscors judged the skirmish to be only an expression of mutual ill wishes. He chose to stay hidden until both groups moved out of sight. Emerging from the rushes, he encountered a single old man, ornately dressed in a robe of Tyrian purple. The dignified, welcoming smile of the old man resolved Perscors's hesitations, and after an exchange of greetings, he gladly accompanied Konai, high priest of the Sethians (as he proved to be), to his tents.

A few hours later, at midday, Perscors was clean, well-fed, and dressed in borrowed Sethian garments. He and his host, with an immediate mutual regard, had postponed explanations. They now sat facing one another, while Konai listened patiently to his guest's selective account of his first day on Lucifer. When Perscors had finished, a long, diplomatic silence followed. Then Konai spoke, reluctantly and in a cautionary tone.

"Olam I have met, and spoken with, several times. He *may* be a man, at least when far off in space and time. Here I think he is a kind of demon, rather than just a man, and a sorcerer. To our west are the followers of Mani, and they honor Olam as a god, or sub-god. Your friend Valentinus I do not recall, nor would I wish to meet him. Between the Mandaeans and the Manichees I am more than weary of the 'Knowing Ones.' "

"I do not know my friend's faith," Perscors mused

aloud. "But then," he added, "I still am not sure of my own."

"This light-bearer's world," Konai said sadly, "once gave off light. Now it is a dark star, lit by a dimming sun. Yet it, like all the cosmos, deserves worship and glory, for the true God created it, meaning it to be good for His children. The curse of our world is that so many deny its creation by the Father."

"Then who made the universe, according to the deniers?"

"A Demiurge, they say. But they all name him differently, and tell a different tale of how he did it, and why. For them, there is no part of the cosmos empty of demons, and indeed, I believe they *have* populated us with demons. They call your Ruha a demoness."

Perscors brooded a while on this and then asked gently: "But what do you call her?"

"An outcast Mandaean woman, probably crazed, certainly a sorceress, but no more than that."

For a long time they sat in silence. Perscors reflected that he was not yet ready to understand and that he must *act* before he could understand. To the west were Olam and Valentinus, and he would have to reach them, but that too could wait. The turbulence in his spirit spoke to him, and he knew he must go to seek the woman. He rose.

"I will go to the heights, to find her again. She and I must speak."

"You risk everything" was Konai's grim but not unfriendly response. "The Mandaeans spread the scandal that she is the woman of Saklas, whom we worship as an angel of God but they deem the Demiurge. Whatever she is, she has been seen with demons, with beings impersonating Saklas."

Perscors felt within him, for the first time in many years, the anguish of contamination, a clear sense of jealousy. He felt the madness of the sensation. Here, on the other side of the universe, he was suffering from jealousy because he had embraced, once, a woman who might be only a phantom. And the jealousy was inspired by rumors that this dubious being was involved also with an angel or demon! Perscors, for a moment, doubted his own sense of reality, and wondered if he had been dreaming ever since he had followed Valentinus into the tower. But the doubt and wonder vanished suddenly in the rage of his desire to see and perhaps to touch the woman again.

With Konai's troubled disapproval, he left the camp of the Sethians. He had refused the offer of a weapon, and even of provisions.

"I am a free man." He laughed. "Free to love my fate. I will burn through."

Konai studied this wanderer's face, for a last time.

"There is only demonic fire in our world," he said. "It is the fire that all those terrible Knowers call Ignorance. There is a demon in you, but much else besides. Though I like you, I will not bless you. I wish you well."

Set upon his road by Konai, Perscors walked through a long, cool afternoon. He headed for the point where the marsh had turned into rocky heights the day before, but the point had vanished. "Not vanished, shifted," he said to himself as he strode on forcefully through what now seemed endless lowlands. He had begun to have an uncanny sense for space and time shifts on Lucifer, and he followed that sense now.

Yet the marshes yielded, not to heights, but to broad, level, dry fields, empty except for their grass and thick clusters of red wildflowers, of a kind he had not seen before. Twilight was coming on, and his sense of being fated to find Ruha began to waver. As the sun set, he came in sight of a dark forest, and when he came up to it in early evening, he hesitated. "With my fortune, I am bound to encounter something or someone meaningful," he said to himself, and so he entered the forest.

CHAPTER **9**

Achamoth

H A L F A N hour later, he lay bruised and bleeding, bound to the bed of Achamoth.

He had found a curious house only a few hundred yards into the wood. Built of black stone, short and oval, the structure was ominous and prison-like, and so overgrown with moss as to be hardly recognizable amid the trees that overhung it. Pushing the door open, he had confronted a majestic titaness of a woman, as tall as himself, with shoulders nearly as broad as his own. She had seemed to him then, as she did now, powerfully ugly but sexually compelling nevertheless. Her robe was black, and evidently was the skin of some wild beast. Her eyes were astonishingly large and almost colorless. The expression with which she awaited him was hungry at best, and perhaps even murderous. He had stood in the doorway, urgently drawn to her, but also very much moved to depart immediately.

That hesitation had been his last freedom down to this bad moment of his bondage. Once he had crossed the threshold, he realized he was trapped. The burly woman's handmaidens appeared on each side of the door, to bolt it behind him. Two more of them stepped out of the shadows behind her. All four were armed with clubs or daggers. His efforts to speak and explain were lost in their assault upon him. The titaness watched, silently and without emotion, as he struck down the two facing him, and the one to his left, but the fourth clubbed him from behind. Then the demoness, with great strength, moved to pinion him as he staggered. Perscors had nearly broken her hold, which even in his fury and sense of danger he felt as erotic, when he was clubbed again. Before he could recover from being stunned, they had dragged him to the bed and chained him face down, and then bound him more securely. He struggled again, only to be clubbed nearly to insensibility. He lay now in anger and pain, helpless to defend himself further.

Turning his head, he brought the titaness into focus. She sat facing him, a few feet from the bed, with her handmaidens standing ranged behind her. He saw that there were now only three, two of them much battered. The missing one, as he was to discover later, he had slain. Days afterward, he was to reflect on how many beings he had killed on the star Lucifer, and he was to think back to this one as a harbinger of much sorrow.

A voice, harsh and haughty, jolted him as though a great bell were tolling a few inches from his head:

"Hear Achamoth, who once was Sophia-Prunikos, youngest of the Aeons in the Pleroma.

"I fell farthest, and into a passion apart from any embrace.

"You came with my enemies, and would have defiled my sanctuary, even as you have defiled Ruha my daughter.

"Your life is forfeit to my women, to die slowly where you are bound."

She rose and departed, leaving her attendants, three slighter but still sinister versions of herself. One of these went to a fire, to heat implements. Another ripped away the Sethian garments from Perscors, cutting him in six places with her dagger while doing so. The third began to flagellate his back and buttocks with a whip of many strands. Exasperated beyond measure with humiliation and suffering, Perscors broke from the bed in a movement so sudden as to seem miraculous even to him. The ropes came apart, and the hand chains tore away from the bedstead. Naked and bloody, his enormous strength magnified many times by his ordeal, he came at his tormentors, swinging the chains still manacled to his wrists. His right chain cut down the woman with the whip, crushing her forehead, while the left chain first blinded and then partly decapitated the dagger wielder. Bellowing and crazed, he closed upon the last woman, who vainly sought to hold him off with a glowing hot iron. Perscors knocked it aside and split open her head with several blows of the right chain, which partly shattered in the last stroke. Still screaming in exultation and blood-madness, he turned to look for Achamoth.

But that demoness was gone, away from his vengeance. His fury continuing, he went from chamber to chamber of the single-story house, slashing at every object with his chains. In the act of breaking apart a metallic caldron, he freed his right wrist from the chain, and staggered to a sudden halt. He stood in what seemed the central chamber, surrounded by wreckage, and employed fragments of ruined vessels to pry his other wrist free. Then he collapsed into a corner, crouched against the wall, breathing in great gasps while his body and spirit descended from madness into something like his ordinary state. He shivered in his nakedness, bleeding in many places, with the greatest hurts on his scalp and in the furrows made upon the whole of his back. His first thought was to vow revenge against Achamoth, whom he would seek before finding Ruha and then going west to his companions.

Reflection altered the sequence of his resolutions. He bathed and tended his wounds as best he could, and then foraged for food and drink amid the chaos of the wrecked rooms. Unable to find other garments, he settled for a loose fur robe of Achamoth's. Wearing her attire, eating her fruits, and drinking her wine, he wandered through her ruined house until in his weariness he knew he must sleep. But he armed himself with a dagger, and with a lance he had found, and kept these at hand as he sank down upon the bed where he had been tortured. In the house of the demoness, he was thrown into a deep sleep.

CHAPTER **10**

The Doctrine of the Limit

MANY DISTANCES to the west, Olam woke up at midnight of his second day on Lucifer. Valentinus had vanished earlier in the day, while they had moved through the lands of the Manichees. But Olam had no concern for the well-being of his experienced disciple, who would turn up again at the appointed time and place, some days hence, as self-reliant as ever. The Promethean Perscors, Olam reflected, would be of concern only if he died prematurely or went thoroughly bad too soon. Olam smiled formidably, his yellow eyes aglow in the night. All beings—whether demons, sorcerers, or men and women—who came in the path of *that* quester would be thoroughly scorched for their misdeeds. "I have let a scourge loose among them." Olam laughed to himself, expecting that even a Demiurge would find this human spirit too much to subdue or contain. But having work of his own to do, Olam turned his will to the night journey awaiting him, a journey toward the place of the being called Horos. This was neither god, demon, nor man, but a living hypostasis, an abstract existence.

The moon would not rise for three hours, but Olam could see in the dark rather better than he could in the day. Sure of foot, he climbed rapidly through heights. Horos spent its existence on a pinnacle in the western mountains. Its presence was shunned equally by the Manichees, living to its east, and by their enemies the Marcionites, living in the valleys to its west. Horos was a voice that neither slept nor ate, a voice that kept watch from its pinnacle. Intruders were met by avalanches.

Olam climbed for nearly three hours. The oval moon rose, throwing a blue-white light, as apparently radiant and unreflected as its own, on the mountains. Olam looked upon the scene, unmoved by its obvious beauty. As he swung himself lithely over a precipice, he gazed ahead at a narrow ridge that would be his pathway to the Place of the Limit, where the pinnacle of Horos was centered. Without surprise, but with intense distaste, Olam saw a figure standing at the midpoint of the ridge. A moment later and he and Saklas confronted one another, a few feet apart over a deep, narrow abyss.

Saklas stood in the moonlight, his azure beauty made more vivid by contrast to the twisted yellow ugliness of Olam. The Demiurge's eyes were luminous, giving forth the same light as the moon of Lucifer. Olam looked down at the bare feet of Saklas, because they were surrounded by seven concentric circles of blue radiance, scored into the stone of the ridge. Between the

Demiurge's feet, one thick black line of shadow ran across the circle, dividing the diagram in half.

"I'm not here to wrestle with you, Saklas. You don't need your diagram as a defense against me."

"The circles are there to keep your evil out of this world's soul" was Saklas's stern reply. His voice sounded with a crystal ring, in fine distinctness to Olam's deep, low growl.

"A splendid device for warding off evil," jeered Olam. "What is that thick black line if it isn't your Gehenna?"

"A Tartarus for demons like you and your sect. What are you doing here?"

"Just what you are doing," Olam mocked. "I am on my way to prefigure a few events or perhaps to see where the balance lies in these parts."

"This time you aren't getting through to the pillar of the Limit." Saklas worked his will on the diagram, which rose up, ring by ring of light, into the air, to advance against his enemy.

Everlasting as his conflicts had been, Olam had no direct experience of this sorcery. Hunched into himself, he waited for the combat.

The first circle came at him in the shape of a lion. As Olam struck a fist in what seemed the face of a golden lion, he saw dissolving before him the face of a being whom he had confronted in battle before, and whom he knew as the Archon Michael.

Next came the bull-shaped Souriel. Olam disdainfully threw the force aside, jabbing his finger at its hot nose. Impatient, Olam moved forward against the oncoming system of Archons. The serpent-shaped Raphael darted against him but was stunned by a two-handed blow. Gabriel, shaped like an eagle, went down as Olam grabbed its wing and whirled the creature around his head until the wing cracked off. There now loomed up against him the bear-shaped Thauthabaoth. But the impetus of the Aeon's forward movement dashed the bear aside, and trampled the dog-shaped Erathaoth, who came on next. The seventh circle, Onoel, screamed at Olam, but the ass-shaped Archon was swept aside in the onrush. Olam came at what should have been Saklas, but it dissolved. The power of his yellow hands held only the blue moonlight. The Demiurge, shaken, had vanished to choose another time and place.

Olam did not pause to exult at his victory in this skirmish but hastened down the ridge to a rocky plateau. Rising out of its midst was a stone pillar, looking from certain angles and distances like a cross and from others like a jagged pinnacle. Horos waited at the top of the pillar, glaring down at the interloper. A shower of rocks descended, coming at Olam seemingly from all directions. Warily he dodged and retreated, until he stood out of range, staring up at the grotesque, ageless figure of the keeper of the Limit.

"You are wasting your energies, you odd wretch, and may give me a useless injury. Answer a few questions only and I will go out of here."

"I know you, Olam" came the querulous reply, in a voice infirm yet piercing. "I do not give knowledge for the asking. This is my place, and mine alone, and I will not be bothered by anyone."

"Peculiar, foul monstrosity! I am here to help you do your work, to keep some spark uncontaminated on this world. Where does Achamoth locate herself? Where is the Topos of the Demiurge? Where have they moved the tower I built among the Manichees?"

A torrent of small rocks whirled down from the plateau, crashing far away from Olam.

"I shall not stir from here until you convey a few facts. You will run out of rocks yet, and then I will climb up there and bother you a bit more closely!"

"Ungrateful monster and demon!" Horos wailed at a high pitch. Suddenly he began to intone a chant of warding-off, which told a story Olam knew too well already. Olam winced and sat down on the rocky ground, knowing he must hear the complaint through, and confident that patience would compel the obsessed voice to answer his question.

"The very last and youngest of the Aeons, Sophia, plunged forward and fell victim to Pathos, to Passion, to Suffering, without the embrace of her consort.

"This Pathos she called Love, but it was Impudence, as she had no such intimacy with the Forefather as she asserted.

"Yet this Pathos is the search for the Father.

"Sophia fell into Achamoth, because of her wish to embrace this greatness.

"Achamoth suffered great distress due to the depth and inscrutability of the Father.

"Achamoth kept pushing on and on and would have been swallowed up by the sweetness of self-satisfaction.

"But I, Horos, am the Power consolidating the cosmos.

"She fell against my Limit, and so was kept at a distance from the sweetness.

"Someday she will push again, be held up again, and will return to herself.

"Her Dark Intention will cease, and she will return to herself."

"A pretty fable," Olam jeered. "Speak it as often as you

want, you feeble oracle, but for now and time to be, I know that she and all other horrors are running loose, here as elsewhere. Tell me where she is, where the Place of the Daemon is, and whereto they have stolen my tower!"

"Achamoth has fled as far as she can," Horos wheezed out. "As for Saklas's place, you will find it when you find her! And of your precious tower, I neither know nor care. Let me be!"

Horos had ended with a scream and stood trembling now, rocking to and fro upon its pillar.

"As far as she can flee," Olam reflected aloud, "and to the Place of the Demiurge. That is probably all the wretch knows. She has only a short start, and I have some days more on this accursed world. West! Due west, and I will find her!"

Without glancing at Horos again, Olam clambered past him, and rapidly began a descent that was a course westward.

CHAPTER **11**

The Way Out and Down: The Battle

IN PAIN and humiliation Perscors woke at dawn of
his third day on Lucifer. As his eyes opened, he saw his
own right hand clenching a lance, and then looked at the
dagger resting in his left one. He rose in that house of
pain, gripping the weapons.

Stiffly, Perscors went toward the door of the house,
but found only another chamber, and then another, all
littered by his fury. He stumbled upon the corpse of the
first of Achamoth's women whom he had killed, but no
door was by her, though it was at her station by the door
that he, with his bare left hand, had destroyed her. His
circuit of the windowless rooms went on, but still no
door appeared. "Sorcery," he cursed, and compelled
himself to remain still.

53

Perscors stared at the chamber's wall, where he stood, and realized that he was staring at himself. The whole of this wall was a mirror, or something like one. A revulsion came upon him as he gazed at the murderous and baffled expression of his own countenance. He felt no identity with the figure he confronted. A dark humor rose in him. At least, he thought, I am hardly idolatrous of—or to— my own shadow. Responding to a drive, he entered the wall, walking into and through his own image, and immediately was thrown downward.

He felt his falling direction as an outward one, and angrily set himself against fear, relaxing his body except for the hands, which held his weapons all the harder. Whatever waited at the end of this sorcery, he vowed to himself, would find in him no helpless victim. His fall through this dark void grew slower and slower, curving outward in great sweeps. Perscors sensed his own weightlessness and prepared his spirit for an end to the long descent.

He came down knees bent, soundlessly and without effort but in total darkness. Unable, after some moments, to distinguish anything around him, he braced himself upon what seemed a smooth stone surface, his lance and dagger at the ready. In only a few minutes he heard the faint but unmistakable clatter of arms somewhere behind him. Swinging around, he saw dim lights at what seemed no great distance, and heard a muffled sound, as if of drums, moving toward him as if echoing the lights.

Another moment and the lights brightened and, crimson against a black horizon, rose, revealing seven advancing figures, masked and lightly armored, each with lance and dagger. Perscors counted them off, noticing as they came closer that the masks were animals' heads. Here on Lucifer, or wherever he now was, Perscors had been coming slowly to realize that his physical strength was increasing, and a lust for battle possessed him as he waited for his masked enemies.

No more than seven yards away, as he judged, they halted at the ready, in a battle line that stationed them about two yards apart. Perscors, his heart pounding in triumphant fury, moved toward them. A few seconds after he began his advance they broke and ran. The lights darkened suddenly, and Perscors, frustrated and angrier still, was left alone in the abyss of blackness.

He stood again and listened. There was a low breathing coming toward him, off to his right. "Animal masks and now an animal!" he muttered silently but an even more inward voice told him not to strike as this beast now trotted toward him, with a yelp that seemed to be one of relief. It came up to him and licked his feet under his robe. Both bewildered and glad, Perscors transferred his dagger to his lance hand, knelt down, and found himself rubbing the head of what seemed a large and very friendly hound. The hound licked his fingers, and Perscors uttered words he half remembered from his childhood: "Prosper your journey, and the angel of God keep you company. So they went forth both, and the young man's dog with them."

Suddenly the hound raised his head and bayed, warning Perscors of danger. Perscors rose, with lance and dagger set, the hound for a companion by his side. The great red lights glared again, and to a drumbeat in a quadruple measure the seven armed men advanced on Perscors, but more warily and hesitantly than the first time. Perscors studied their animal masks, from left to right: lion, bull, snake, eagle, bear, dog, ass. The dog mask grotesquely combined the features of hound and wolf. Perscors spared a moment to study his own hound, whose large sympathetic eyes beamed back at him, as fearless as Perscors felt himself to be. A rage at all his mishaps surged again in Perscors, and he charged at the adversary line, his lance raised and his hound charging by his side.

The masked beings wavered, but this time held, and each wing circled in so as all but to surround Perscors as he charged. They ringed him, their armor flashing like fire. Perscors's eyes glared a darker fire, for he was swifter and stronger than what opposed him. One lance came close enough to tear Achamoth's robe, but by then Perscors had thrust his own dagger into the heart of the one masked as a bear. Unable to retrieve either weapon, Perscors seized the serpentine one by the throat and broke his neck with a sharp tear downward to the right. The crimson gleam of fire was all about him as he dodged another lance and broke a hand that slashed him with its dagger. Amid the screams surrounding him, Perscors made out the furious baying of his hound and started toward it. Literal fire seemed to have broken out, and the lion-man ran past Perscors, shouting in agony, pulling vainly at his mask, which was crackling with flame. Into Perscors's path rushed another tormented, howling enemy, tearing at a mask so full of fire as to be unrecognizable. Perscors kicked the creature aside and came up to the body of the hound, run through by a lance, but with its fangs still sunk into the groin of the dog-man's corpse.

Nothing living was near Perscors as he stood and grieved, at the center of a ring of waning fire. For the first time on Lucifer, his sorrow had crept beyond the circle of his self. Yet he glanced at the bodies of his enemies and did not count them, feeling only contempt toward the fallen. Day of some sort had come to the underground world of Lucifer, and a pale, reddish, un-sunlit sky was above him. He turned dully away from his hound to what he sensed was west and began to walk forward over the smooth stones. For a moment he thought of retrieving a weapon, but then shrugged the thought away. Bare-handed, he felt himself to be over-matched with anything this world could send against him, below or aboveground. The fires burned away into the stones, and Perscors shook with the cold pink of the day-glare, as he marched forward to his heimarmene.

CHAPTER **12**

The Way Out and Down: Ruha

TIME ITSELF seemed to have fled away; Perscors had no notion of how long he had marched. The stones had turned to black soil, except where the ground gaped open, revealing nothing but an endless abyss. Skirting one of these fissures, Perscors saw for the first time in this underworld some growth. Along the fissure's edge he found a clump of milky flowers, stark white in their dark setting. Drawn to them, he tried to pull one up, but was amazed at the root's resistance. Crouching down, he struggled obstinately and some moments later finally drew out the black root. So great was the fatigue caused by the root's obduracy that he felt more drained than he had been by the battle. The plant gave off an unpleasant odor, strong and garlicky, but he felt comforted by it and placed it in the right-hand pocket of his torn robe.

58

As he strode on, vegetation began to appear in the form of clumped shrubs, sparse at first, but progressively thicker, until indeed their presence started to slow his pace. He moved through darkened groves of cypress trees, illuminated obscurely by the reddish light from above. Abruptly, Perscors faced a vast lake sunk in deep shadow; nearby yawned the wide mouth of a rocky cavern. He did not hesitate but advanced into it.

He now moved along in complete darkness, until he rounded a turning, and would have stumbled but for an inner voice again slowing him down. The giant eddy of a whirlpool churned below him, emitting light, but only in sudden bursts. A winding path led down to his left, and Perscors followed it, slowly and uncertainly, because of the flickering of the light. After he had descended through many windings, he saw more clearly; a huge river coursed before him at the end of the turnings and, despite the strength of its motion, gave off a steadier gleam. With a sense of return, Perscors made his way down to the river. The image of Ruha rose within him, for he seemed to have come back to her realm, while actually before him stood two figures over by the river, momentarily compelling him to break away from his dream of the woman.

Two bearded men of almost his own height confronted him. Both were in black armor, though unmasked, and neither bore a weapon; their dark, languid faces, not identical, almost rhymed with each other. Princely in their bearing, they awaited him without expression, yet their eyes were intent upon him.

Perscors felt only impatience and angry curiosity as he stared back at these apparent nobles. He did not wait for them to speak. "My name is Perscors. I have had many misadventures. I seek either directions out of here, to the world above, or else information that will take me to a woman named Ruha."

One of the black armored beings replied in a tone of disdain: "I am Urpel; this is Marpel, my brother. We are princes of the earth of Siniavis, which is this region of the underworld. There will be no woman for you here."

Marpel, after a silence, spoke also: "You are not welcome here. There is blood for which you are accountable, but you are not our concern. We will neither help you nor attack you. Go from us."

His now characteristic rage possessed Perscors, and almost without willing it, he rushed at the brothers. Though they cried aloud for aid in high, piercing, effeminate voices, no one came, and their struggle was brief. In a few seconds, Perscors had crushed the face of Urpel and broken Marpel's neck. He felt no remorse but only a continued frustration, a kind of rage against meaninglessness.

He exchanged the torn robe of Achamoth for the black armor of Marpel, and felt relief at shedding her garment. On impulse, he transferred the milky flower with its black root to his left gauntlet. He wished that he were equipped with a weapon, and twenty paces down the riverbank, he discovered the short thick swords of his princely victims. With one in each hand, and the need to find the woman Ruha, he marched down along the darkened river of light, convinced that his fate would bring him to her.

At the river's turn, a man stood waiting for him. The murderous intensity of his quest left Perscors as he came up to this beautiful being—tall and with fair straight hair falling to his shoulders—who stood clothed in azure robes and who emanated an aura of blue-white radiance. Saklas the Demiurge smiled a welcome to Perscors, who found himself kneeling at the feet of this apparent angel of light, his uncrossed swords falling with a muffled sound into the dust as if before an exalted presence.

"I am Saklas, who made this world upon which you trespass.

"The two who carried you here seek to teach you their evil.

"I am immutable, and I imitate the Father as best I can.

"Do not consider that my world is badly made, only because there is so much sorrow and pain in it.

"The Aeon who brought you refuses immortality to the entire heaven and all the stars.

"Why does Olam care to inhabit the copy of a world that he hates?

"Believe in your own fire, embrace your own fate, and you will come home to me."

The high crystal tone of the Demiurge's voice died away, and Saklas vanished from the sight of Perscors, who rose to his feet and repossessed the two swords. He was greatly bewildered. One impulse urged him to find his way back to the surface in order to reach Valentinus, and to be able to decide truly which side of this violent struggle was his own. But a deeper force drove him along the river that he might learn what his relation to the woman was to be.

It was only a few moments later that she was coming toward him, across a blue meadow. Her smile was disdainful, yet less so, he thought, than it had been when they had embraced. He walked with her, feeling the brutal dullness of his black armor near her green robe, yet he did not let go of the two swords. Around them, the caverns had become gardens again, gardens flourishing under a light which turned the deep green of shading foliage into the blackness of cast shadow or of what had been burned, gardens fit for Proserpina as the Queen of Hell in an old legend.

They passed through the arbor with its silver couch, on which they had embraced, but Ruha walked on, frowning for a moment, or so he thought. Despite his desire, he began to feel his weariness, thirst, and hunger; he wondered how long it was since he had moved into and through his own image in Achamoth's mirror.

Then Perscors abruptly stopped, and spoke to Ruha: "I need to rest and to eat and drink. Have you no words?"

Her voice was low, intense, and to him wholly compelling: "We go to feast close by."

She walked on, looking straight ahead, and he saw that she would say no more, for now. Perscors hesitated, but then realized he must go with her. Between the hesitation and the resolve, a vertigo of sight had begun for him, and he was stunned to disbelief by what he now saw. Though he still stood where he had stopped, he also was walking on ahead, by her side. He looked down, in great alarm. There was the black armor and the sword in each hand. He looked ahead again, and there he strode, in black armor by her green robe and her black hair, and the striding Perscors that he saw carried a sword in each hand. Either he watched his double walking with Ruha, or he himself was that double, and what watched him was something other than himself.

He thought back to Achamoth's mirror. What he saw getting farther ahead of him, with Ruha, was that reflec-

tion of himself through which he had then passed. Had
he entered it? Or was he now that reflection, looking on
at the active figure who had passed through him? Would
he, or his image, or both, get back to the world above?
And in any case, had he lost himself to his image? His
heart pounding with anxieties, he began to run after
Ruha and the being by her side.

But he could not catch up, however fast he ran,
though Ruha and the other Perscors continued to walk
steadily; as in a dream, the distance increased the more
rapid his efforts. In exhaustion, Perscors fell upon the
river path. His left gauntlet slipped off and he saw that
the harsh, black-rooted, milky flower was not there. Had
he lost it, or was it in his double's gauntlet? "How long
do you mean to be content?" a voice whispered to him,
and he remembered one meaning of the sight of one's
double—that its appearance preceded death. Perscors
struggled to his feet, fearing not for himself but for his
double, whose end was so close.

With renewed energy, Perscors hastened down the
river path. It baffled him that so much time had elapsed
and yet there was still no sight of Ruha and his other
self. The river grew wilder. Perscors glanced off to his
right and saw Ruha and her lover, a good distance across
the meadow, moving toward a house of smooth yellow
stone. He watched them enter, as he ran toward them.

It did not surprise him, as he came up to the house,
that a walk around it revealed no door. On his second
circuit, he observed an oval window halfway up one wall
of the house. How to climb twenty feet of smooth stone
seemed beyond his reckoning; yet his curiously increased strength and agility, particularly in this underworld, had added to his natural daring. Even if he could

not save his double, he wished to behold this fate that was somehow both his own and that of another.

A close survey of the walls revealed almost enough overgrowth of vine to carry him up to the ominously lone window, provided the vine held. Perscors left his swords below and scrambled up, but with great difficulty. The window proved to be of opaque crystal. In another sudden fury, Perscors kicked at it. Without shattering, it swung open, and he lowered himself into a bare chamber. This led to a long passageway onto a balcony, overlooking a banqueting room below, built as a kind of amphitheater. So many voices were rising from below—laughing, screaming, singing—that Perscors believed himself to be unheard. He crept along the balcony until he could peer down. His first sight startled him with revulsion, but he compelled himself to stare long and steadily at a medley of grouped sexual couplings and tortures. In the midst, the other Perscors aggressively participated, roaring in exultation.

CHAPTER **13**

The Way Out and Down: Defilement

F O R   A   while, Perscors was able to watch, focusing
with ambivalent fascination upon the group at the center, comprising Ruha, his apparent self, and two atten-
dant women who resembled her, though each was
slighter and less glowing than her mistress. While
Perscors's double was spontaneous and exuberant in his
movements, totally abandoned in both active and passive
postures, Ruha and her women were expressionless and
seemed rehearsed or ritualistic in every gesture and
every act. The three women in turn bent down before
the lustful double, each draping her arms about the
necks of the other two, and presenting herself for pene-
tration. While these cycles of substitutions went slowly

on, they exchanged places in scourging, and being scourged by, him.

Abruptly, Perscors moved back from the balcony to the passageway, unable to sustain more of the scene. From the fire of ignorance he had passed to the air of grief, and he could not order his thoughts or feelings. Whatever was to happen to his double might happen without his observation, though a sense of foreboding lingered in him. Toward Ruha, he did not know what he felt, and he could not be jealous of his own shadow or blame his other self for the setting or nature of the ritual orgy. But what was the cause of the profound sadness that pervaded him? Rather than confront his own double, he would not enter that revel, and only an escape upward seemed a possible release from the sorrow of a spectacle that was more than that, even if it placed him back in the violent activity of the house of Achamoth.

"Or have I ever left that house?" he said aloud. Without intending it, he had gone down the passageway beyond the empty chamber of his entrance, and he came now to a vast room so different that it seemed to be in some other structure. A kind of octagonal courtroom, was his first impression, but when he looked again, it seemed more like a chapel or meetinghouse. Because the light was so dim, he only gradually saw a shrouded form standing behind a lectern. Facing him, Perscors moved closer, but stopped halfway, some yards from the shrouded figure, who fixed his eyes upon Perscors and began to chant in a voice so strong that it overflowed the huge hall with thunderous resonance: "Perscors! How do you think your trial will end?"

Awed when he heard his name, Perscors changed to a

state of anger at the question. "I do not know who you are, though you know me! And where and how am I on trial? Who dares to try me?"

"You are not fit to learn my name. Nor can it do you good. The Archons try you even as you burn here in your ignorance."

"Try me for *what*?" Perscors roared back.

"Can you not *see* anything at all? Your self is below, and by now it feasts its fill upon the flesh of one of Ruha's women. They have drugged you into their horror."

Perscors vowed silently that he would depart from this world of darkness.

"Depart? Yes, your spark can go, but your soul they will execute here. Go back, without understanding, to the den of Achamoth, but look in no more mirrors, for your shadow self, your psyche, is gone from you."

"Who are you?" Perscors burst out.

"Yet another messenger, another stranger to whom you will not listen. Go from me, or accept some instruction before you come to judgment. You, who cannot see two steps in front of you!"

"Judgment? Judgment?" Perscors laughed with a force paining his chest and throat. "What can judgment mean, whether on or below the star Lucifer? The star *has* been judged, and existence itself is a punishment here!"

The shrouded voice altered tone: "*Some* knowledge evidently you have attained. But listen!

"In the name of the great Life! I cry to you, I instruct you.

"I will tell you of the worlds of Darkness, and what is said in them.

"Beyond the earth of Light downward and beyond that earth outward is the earth of Darkness.

"That earth is black water and its depths are caverns of gloom.

"From the black water, Saklas the King of Darkness was fabricated through the passion of Achamoth and the evil of his own nature, and came forth.

"His Darkness grew strong and multiplied through demons, devils, genii, spirits, hmurthas, Liliths, temple-and-chapel spirits, idols, Archons, angels, vampires, goblins, noxious sprites, imps of anxiety, monsters, elves of nets and locks, and Satans, all the detestable modes of Darkness of every form and type, male and female of Darkness; clumsy, gloomy, rebellious, furious, raging, stubborn, poisonous, foolish, lazy, abominable, filthy and stinking. Some among them are deaf, dumb, mute, stupid, stuttering, unhearing, perplexed, ignorant. Some among them are insolent, violent, hotheaded, shrill, debauched, irascible, children of blood, attended by flashing fire, makers of devastating conflagration: do you not hear your nature in these words the Great Life has sent me to speak? And some among them are and will be sorcerers, forgers, liars, swindlers, robbers, deceivers, exorcists, false oracles, soothsayers. All these together are master builders of every abomination, inaugurators of oppression who commit murder and shed blood with no compassion or pity. These are the artists of every hideous rite. The taste of their lips is like trees of gall and poison, the sap of their bodies is like naphtha and pitch."

Perscors stood in silence. Then he asked of the shrouded messenger: "What of the woman Ruha?"

The great voice of the Shroud came forth again:

"Ruha the Holy Archdemoness: daughter of Achamoth; sister of Saklas.

> Her mind is malice, replete with lies.
> She is full of sorcery,
> Full of witchcraft and false wisdom.
> Ruha sits there with her hmurthas,
> Amulet-spirits masking as handmaidens.
> There she sits and practices false magic.
> Who gave the liar instruction?
> Who called her the Holy Spirit?"

For Perscors, it was enough, and more than enough. He turned and fled the vast vault of the room. But where was there release for him from this underground realm? He had descended through his reflection: he sensed that the voyage back also must involve his shadow self. Stealthily, he went back upon the balcony and peered down into the now quiet amphitheater.

Ruha sat enthroned, naked and triumphant, in the midst of the company, upon a silver dais. Saklas stood off at her left side, one of her women at her right. The other Perscors lay bound in chains at her feet. Whether dazed or drugged, he seemed lost in a stupor. Next to him lay the corpse of Ruha's other woman, mutilated, with terrible deep ridges torn into her flesh. On every side, the former revelers were massed expectantly. Drumbeats began to reverberate, and the crowd parted to allow a masked, hunched figure to make his way up to the bound Perscors. With astonishment, Perscors himself, crouched above, read in the color and folds of the mask a parody of the yellow, grinning countenance of Olam.

Ruha addressed her assembly, in a high, clear voice:

"This murderous wanderer has slain my hmurtha, who sought only to give him pleasure.

"He tore and devoured her flesh. He lies there bestially drunk upon the blood of her body.

"He came with the Knowing Ones. Olam brought him; let Olam destroy him!"

As the drumbeats increased, the creature masked as Olam knelt down, encircled the throat of Perscors's double with a necklace of iron hands, and strangled him to death.

Perscors returned to the passageway from the balcony. An overwhelming sense of defilement possessed him. It was a fury to him that his reflected self should have died so helplessly; he was filled with a rage against every being on or under Lucifer. He returned to the bare room, went out through its oval window, and lowered himself by vines to the ground. With a sword in each hand again, he took up his stance near the stone house, determined to slaughter all its occupants when they emerged.

He glanced down at his feet. In front of him lay the milky flower with its black stem. After he had replaced it in his gauntlet, he began to be conscious of change. He looked ahead and immediately saw that the stone house was gone. It took him a few moments to realize that he was staring once again at a mirror, for the reflection given back to him was only of the wall behind him, in the house of Achamoth.

CHAPTER **14**

Hermas, the Eye of Fire

VALENTINUS EXAMINED the temple grounds spread out in the valley below him. Night was coming on, but Valentinus was in no haste to descend. He hoped first to remember just a little more, since he needed to consult an oracle precisely on his difficulties in remembering. But he despised oracles and felt particular scorn for the temple of Hermas, to which he had come.

Memory had been failing in him for a long time. He slept little, because he could not bear his nightmares. In the few hours he had slept since being on Lucifer, he had dreamed again what he knew was a recurrent dream. In this, he wandered in the muddy world of the Kenoma, a wilderness of emptiness and desolation. There, amid the mud, he saw gold shining forth. He ran through the muddy void as rapidly as he could, but when he came up to the gold, he found instead a newly born male child lying peacefully in the mud. The baby spoke, trying to utter his name, but the language was unknown to Valentinus.

"Tell me your name so that I can know," Valentinus implored. Frowning, the baby spoke again incomprehensibly, and then sank into the mud. Valentinus woke from the dream even as he dug frantically through the mud, unable to locate either gold or child.

Poised above the temple grounds, Valentinus prepared to go down. He had left Olam, knowing they would meet in the West, but sensing that Olam's presence made his difficulties with memory still greater. Had he been on Lucifer before? Olam clearly had; yet Valentinus had encountered no recognizable places so far, and he suspected that the star was new to him. But a troubled sense of repetition afflicted him, as well as a fear that he had exposed Perscors to dangers in order that he, Valentinus, might recall experiences he had lost.

The temple compound was protected by a high outer wall. There was a light in the gate, and Valentinus moved down toward it. As he came up to the gate, three armed priests of Hermas blocked his path. With three lances only a few feet away from his chest, Valentinus stopped and stood quietly. His pale, semi-albino face was expressionless, and he made no reply to the challenges of the priests. Though unarmed, he was not a person the priests felt safe in attacking. Two remained on guard, while the third fell back to consult authority.

Basilides, high priest of Hermas, came to the gate. A shrewd glance at Valentinus persuaded him of his visitor's importance. He waved away the armed priests and invited Valentinus in with signs of elaborate courtesy. Facing the high priest during the subsequent meal of welcome, Valentinus ate sparingly and in silence of the roast lamb before him.

They sat afterward, in the cool of the evening, in the high priest's garden. After an hour had passed in silent meditation, the host abruptly began a chant:

"Poimandres, Shepherd of men, the Mind of the Absolute, comes to whosoever he will and speaks his Word.

"Rolling and twisting, a fearful darkness appears, forcing its way down. The serpent of Darkness falls into a humid nature, a confusion, giving off smoke, and uttering a lament.

"The lament is a cry sounding like the voice of fire.

"Out of the Light a holy Word mounts over the humid nature, the sludge, to the heights. Primal Man is that Word.

"Poimandres is that Light. That which in you sees and hears is the Word I speak."

The high priest broke off and gazed at Valentinus long and intently.

Somberly and hesitantly, Valentinus spoke as if he were bringing forward a trouble long held back in his being: "Something of this beginning I have heard. My differences with you come after the beginning."

"Why have you sought us out? We wish no trouble with Olam. We fight no battles with him."

"A knowledge tells me that you have an art of memory. I think Olam has brought me to this world that I might remember, but nothing as yet has come back to me. Have you seen me before?"

"Never. But I have seen someone who had the look of you, who came with Olam. Three came together that

time; one was like you, but the other was a raging warrior who died against the Manichees. Or so they said,
but they lie freely. He may have died much farther in
the West."

"What art of memory have you?"

The high priest shook his head decisively. "For such a
one as yourself, no art will serve. But try the favor of
Hermas. Go at midnight to the Eye of the Fire, and
perhaps the Mind will speak to you. There is nothing
else we can offer."

The high priest rose, a little coldly, and departed.
Valentinus settled himself to meditation, knowing that a
priest would come for him at midnight. But the meditation yielded to sleep, almost immediately, and to another
dream of the Kenoma.

There in the great void, Perscors marched through the
muddy wastes. He wore black armor and carried two
swords. Waiting for him were three ranks of armed men.
Between Perscors and his enemies loomed up a figure
that seemed to resemble Olam. Perscors charged past
him at the waiting enemy. Striking from behind, the
Olam-like figure cut Perscors down by a blow to the
neck with a huge hammer. The armed men trampled the
corpse of Perscors into the mud, while the figure appear-
ing to be Olam shouldered his hammer and strode away.

This scene drifted by, and Valentinus saw himself
walking up to the dishonored body of his friend. Bending over the corpse, he beheld again not Perscors but the
speaking newborn babe, smiling now and uttering a
name unlike any other. But the babe dissolved into the
mud, and Valentinus woke to his recurrent torment of
forgetfulness.

He walked in the garden until, at midnight, a priest

came to conduct him to the compound's innermost shrine. The guide left him at the door of the pavilion. Valentinus unhesitatingly entered a dark chamber and walked forward. He paused; a flame broke forth some six feet before him, and then above the flame there flared forth an Eye of Fire, the size of a man's head. Valentinus, little impressed, stared at the Eye and said nothing. The Eye of Fire regarded him a while and then suddenly burned away.

A voice, weary and petulant, whispered to Valentinus, a few inches away from his left ear: "Heresiarch, you fell away from the old gods of your people. What do you expect from the priest of Thoth?"

"What gods?" Valentinus asked, with great bitterness. "And why the Egyptian Thoth? Because Hermas is a name for Thoth? And what people? What have I to do with Egypt?"

The voice whispered again, with increased petulance: "Six times, on six spheres, your material body has dissolved. Six times you have left your character to the demons.

"Six times you have pressed up through the system of spheres. In the first sphere you left your ability to wax and wane; in the second your cunning; in the third sphere your desire for possession; in the fourth your overbearing boastfulness; in the fifth your rashness; in the sixth your need for power.

"You strive upward for the seventh time. Leave behind the malicious lie against the Demiurge and you will possess only your true strength. Then you may enter the eighth world . . ."

The whisper ceased; the Eye of Fire flamed forth again. Valentinus, more bitter than before, called out against the Eye: "Yours is the malice of falsehood. I have slipped six knots, loosed six bonds, removed six garments. But the seventh knot fastens the soul, and it is the knot of your lying Demiurge, who calls himself the Mind of God. When my spark ignites the seventh knot, I will rise up in my own strength. For I have come to know myself, and I have collected myself from everywhere, and I have not sown children to the Archon but have uprooted his roots and have collected the dispersed members, and I know you who you are: for I am of those from above."

The Eye burned out again. Valentinus swung about, left the shrine, and, looking straight ahead, marched through the compound of Hermas. He did not stop at the outer gate but kicked against it. The priests guarding the gate watched it fall open as Valentinus strode out into the night. He set his face to the west, and confidently moved against the darkness.

CHAPTER **15**

Nekbael

PERSCORS SHATTERED the mirror with a double blow, both swords slashing as one. He turned and found the door to Achamoth's house. With all his force, he pushed against it and went out into the forest. Though he sensed that his path might lead him to Ruha again and again, his impulse was to seek out Valentinus and Olam. He wandered westward through the wood.

More aware than before that he was neither beast nor god, Perscors felt his solitude. Pondering with his own sad heart, gazing at the boundless forest, he wished he could pray for a sign, but he was acutely conscious of his spiritual confusion. The shadows, as he walked, were everywhere, though it was broad day. His solitude had no part in fear, but he understood that much of his

power was identical with the dark flame of his ignorance.

The forest seemed merely blank extension: wide, deep,
long, and endless tangle. Against it, Perscors set his
slowly clarifying love of his own fate. His shadow self,
which he could not bear to define, had died in shame, in
a realm out of this maze and down from it. But his sense
of identity had survived, and he felt again a confidence
that he was on the star Lucifer to some purpose. He kept
on.

After an hour he saw a phantasm. The form of a
woman, red-haired and tall, floated momentarily above
the trees. Perscors judged it to be a premonitory image,
an indication that he was not fated to wander on without
further misadventure. He had not long to wait, for only a
few moments after seeing the apparition he came upon a
clearing in the forest.

A veiled woman sat alone. She was tall and red-haired,
but not, he thought, the woman of the vision. There had
been menace in the phantasm, but not in this figure. He
placed both swords upon the ground and then approached her slowly. As he came up to her, she raised
her veil and laid aside a stole from her shoulders.
Perscors beheld a countenance that seemed to shine as
brightly as the sun he had left behind him on earth, and
not like the dimmed sun of Lucifer. The shady clearing
seemed flooded in sunshine; the shadows of the forest
receded.

But some touch of doubt prevented Perscors from addressing this radiant woman. Though she smiled directly
at him, she too showed a disinclination to speak. He
studied her closely, returning her smile, yet experiencing
a sense of confusion. Her rich robes were forest-green, as

were her boots and her discarded veil and stole. A necklace of heavy yellow gold encircled her throat. She wore
a single ring, with a large black gem, on her left hand.
Though he was not as moved as he had been by his first
sight of Ruha, who instantly and even now seemed at the
center of his cosmic fate, Perscors felt a less ambivalent
if also less intense attraction to this woman. Yet his rapt
perusal of her face made him gradually aware that he
seemed to see two faces at once. Irregular features that
had a piercing aura, compelling fascination by astonish-
ing contrasts, were suddenly replaced by hesitant,
symmetrical features, curiously clear, fresh, restful, uni-
fied. Baffled by this alternation, Perscors felt the necessity
of declaring his name and origin, if only to assure this
remarkable being that he was a man and not a demon.

To his great shock, he could not speak. Her smile had
turned to a look of grave regard, still benign, and she
maintained her silence. Perscors realized that to speak he
must avert his gaze from her, but the interplay of her
wholly disparate faces was too much of an enchantment
for him to look away. At first he felt what seemed the
humor of his situation, standing there helpless to speak
in front of this beautiful being, who continued to sit and
to exchange a grave staring with him. But as his dilemma continued, a growing state of alarm dominated
him. Minutes passed into hours, and still he was rapt,
still speechless. It became clearer to him that he had
stumbled upon sorcery, and that he was in danger, absurd as such an awareness at first seemed. He summoned
his formidable will, that he might either turn his head or
speak, but he failed. Night came on, but the woman's
radiance only increased, and his enthrallment to her features continued. A familiar fury gathered within him.

As his anger mounted, he gradually realized that the unbroken mutual staring was beginning to petrify his limbs. Paralyzed, unable even to flex his muscles or move a hand or foot, he felt the slowly increasing dead weight of his body. All the strength of his soul could not arrest the hideous change he was experiencing. As the night stretched on, he came to understand that only the power of his anger, the fire of his ignorance, could save him. He concentrated his pride in that power toward the moment of the dawn, knowing that either he would break the enchantment then or else he would perish. Throughout all this battle of the spirit, the paralyzing interchange of glances maintained itself. Despite his anger, the frightening and painful pleasure of admiring both her faces was constant.

Just before dawn, his anger failed him. Perscors felt the oblivion of stone. Who could love such a fate? Unable to break the spell of her stare, he realized that he must *listen*. He listened, he concentrated all the remnants of his being upon listening, but no call came. In the dull torpor of the rising sun, Perscors approached what he took to be the waning moments of his existence.

Then it began as a rustling in the treetops, so that he thought he heard the wind. Bit by bit, he knew that he heard his own name being called. It was repeated from all sides of the sky and the forest; then he realized, very slowly, that he was staring at vacancy. The woman was gone, and the deadness began to go from his limbs. His name reverberated all about him, and then ceased. Shaking desperately, moaning his own name to himself, he lay upon the grass. Without hearing it spoken, he began to moan another name: "Nekbael. Nekbael." When he understood that this must be the name of the enchantress, he ceased to moan, and with great difficulty he made himself rise and stagger back to where he had placed his swords. He collapsed next to them, and even as he felt their hilts in his hands, he fell into a saving sleep of total exhaustion.

CHAPTER 16

The Manichees: Doctrine

PERSCORS WOKE in late afternoon, to find himself surrounded by an encampment. He had been left undisturbed and unguarded, his weapons in his hands. Only a small boy had been assigned to watch him and to bring him to the chief of this wandering clan when he awoke.

Following the child through the camp, Perscors puzzled over the nature of this peculiar-looking people. Tall and willowy, they seemed set apart from the other inhabitants of Lucifer that he had encountered, including the men and women of the netherworld.

Herakleides, headman of the "True" or "Elect" among the Manichees, greeted Perscors suspiciously, in front of a large green tent. A dull green was the only color visible anywhere in the camp, whether on the armored soldiers or on the few women and children. The disproportion between the many hundreds of warriors and the few score women and children surprised Perscors, but nearly every outward aspect of these people was startling. After his identity and his relation to Olam had been established, Perscors saw that the suspicious unease of Herakleides had been increased. The only relief that the headman manifested was at Perscors's refusal to declare himself an adherent of the religious outlook of Olam or of anyone else. Concerning his uncanny descent into the underworld, Perscors kept silent.

After a spare supper of vegetables, Herakleides led Perscors for a walk toward the edge of the meadow, just out of hearing of the bowmen posted as guards. Perscors's curiosity resulted in his abandoning some of his newly developed reserve.

"Why do your people look down on the ground wherever they walk?"

"When someone walks on the ground, he injures the Light mixed in with the earth, even as he who moves his hand injures the air."

Perscors stared hard at Herakleides and protested: "But then all action whatsoever is sin!"

"So indeed it is," Herakleides gruffly agreed. Silence ensued.

"But who can live like that? You are surrounded by your soldiers. When you command them to fight, are you urging them to sin?"

Herakleides motioned Perscors to be silent and to listen. Stepping back, the headman began to declaim, in a quietly controlled but very urgent tone of voice:

"We follow Mani, who revealed the mystery of the

Light and the Darkness, the mystery of the great war stirred up by the Darkness against the Light. The beginnings were in the depth of the Darkness, and not in the heights, as Olam asserts. The Darkness desired its better, not out of love for the Light, but out of resentment. The Light loved peace, and so made the soul of man as a sacrifice to the Darkness."

"Then your God of Light is a coward," Perscors retorted. "I have no use for a cowardly god!"

Herakleides smiled savagely. "You are a strong ignorance, a mockery of Primal Man. Olam has not been able to teach you his half truths, and how then shall I teach you the full Word? For what are you but a shadow of the First Creation that the Light, Father of Greatness, sent against the Darkness?"

"What happened to that First Creation?" Perscors asked, somewhat chastened.

"Before the cosmos, there was the Primal Man. When he was called forth, he girded himself with an armor of five kinds: the light breeze, the strong wind, the light, the water, and the fire. With the fire as his lance, he plunged speedily down from the Paradises until he reached the corner of the battlefield."

"That first man was no coward," Perscors remarked somberly, anticipating a tale of defeat, even as he felt an identity with the pre-cosmic warrior.

Herakleides looked more favorably at Perscors. The headman's voice softened and a note of lament came into his declamation:

"The Great Father Himself could not lower His Light to the battle, and so He honored us by sending man in His place. But the Archdevil also had his five kinds: the smoke; the dark fire, consuming; the night of darkness;

the scorching wind; the heavy fog of waters. Armed with these, the King of Darkness went forth to meet Primal Man in battle. When he saw man, the Archdevil brooded and said: 'What I sought far off, I have found close by.' They struggled in the battle for many hours and man was defeated."

Perscors felt a rush of fury, an ancient call to battle, and cried out: "No! Man cannot be defeated!"

"It was wholly a defeat, but as a sacrifice it began our salvation. For the Primal Man, in defeat, gave himself and his five kinds as food to the five kinds of the Archdevil, just as a man who has an enemy mixes a deadly poison into a cake and gives it to him. When the Sons of Darkness had devoured them, the five luminous kinds were devoid of understanding, and the Primal Man became like someone who has been bitten by a mad dog or serpent. Thus the five parts of Light became mixed with the five parts of Darkness."

Herakleides ended in great sadness, his face dead pale against the twilight. Perscors realized that except for the soldiers, women, and children, the Manichees were unusually pale. A drawn face always identified the True or Elect among them.

Herakleides stared at Perscors's black armor, and then spoke very slowly: "I have seen no such armor on Lucifer. Where did you steal the armor of the Sons of Darkness?"

"I took it when I found it," Perscors said shortly. "Armor means so much to you because of the first man's five lost kinds; is that it?"

Herakleides nodded. "The five kinds were both armor and escort to the Primal Man, and they are held captive now. The Archdevil took man's armor and gave it to the

Archons of Darkness. *They ate of his armor,* which means that they devoured man's soul."

Perscors looked down at his armor. Its origins no longer interested him; it was his. And it was not his fire as gorged by demons and then returned to him. It was *his* fire.

Herakleides broke in upon him, as though able to divine his thoughts: "You do not know, despite all your calamities, that you are numb and scarcely conscious, poisoned by having been given as poison. What are you, warrior, except sin, guilt, and error?"

Perscors held back his fury. Very quietly he returned to an earlier question: "What are your own warriors?"

A hostile silence ensued. Wearily, Herakleides renewed explanations: "It is best to *do* nothing. But that is for the true group, for our Elect. Our believers are hearers or soldiers, who acquire merit by making it possible for the Elect to survive. There are only these three: Elect, soldiers, and sinners. It is for you to choose whether you are soldier or sinner."

Perscors was not much impressed. "I have learned that the three were those of the spark, those of the soul, and those of the flesh, and that I was in the second. But I begin to think that these divisions do not matter."

"From what wisdom do you assert you speak?" Herakleides demanded.

"I have found nothing on this world yet that I can trust. Olam came here for his own purposes, to thwart or baffle the Demiurge. Valentinus came to remember who and what he had been. I came, I now understand, to rebeget myself, to become man. But I become only more bewildered. Yet you offer me only a second-best, to be a soldier defending a wholly passive good. I did not come here for that."

Both men were silent. Herakleides felt again a profound uneasiness at the continued presence of Perscors. He spoke decisively: "We will give you shelter tonight. But you must decide by dawn. If you will not serve the Word, then go from us in peace."

Perscors shook his head. "I will depart now."

CHAPTER 17

The Manichees: Dreams before Battle

P E R S C O R S ,   V E R Y late that night, fell asleep in the woods, several hours' march from the camp of the Manichees. Two dreams called to him in the course of the night.

Nekbael, her red hair shining in the darkness, came to him, but on earth, rather than on Lucifer. It was night in the town where he had been born and raised, a summer night on the town green. The lights were out in all the houses when the sorceress approached Perscors. As she came close, he saw only the one face: symmetrical, at peace, almost innocent. She took him by the hands and spoke urgently to him, but in words he could not understand. He cried out in the dream, in the same unknown language, and she faded from him. In her place stood Ruha, mocking and desirable, chanting a litany:

"The son of the King of Darkness spoke to the daughters of Darkness.

"He cried: 'Give me your sons and daughters and I shall make for you the figure of your desire.'

"They brought them and gave them to him.

"He ate the female ones and handed over the males to Nekbael, his companion.

"He entered Nekbael.

"Nekbael became pregnant and bore a son named Adam and a daughter named Havva.

"When Adam woke, he found himself mingled with and imprisoned in everything that exists, shackled in the stench of darkness.

"Then Adam glanced upward and wept, raising his voice powerfully like a lion roaring.

"Woe unto you, Perscors, son of Adam, with your soul shackled, and enslaved to the Archons."

She finished her mockery and embraced him, falling with him onto the green. With Ruha's lips biting cruelly into his left cheek, Perscors roared himself awake, to find himself alone in the forest, the stars above him shining down in their mockery. He would have struck them with his swords if he could. He turned upon his side, away from their insulting glare, and instantly fell into a deeper dream.

He wandered in the waste places, in the void of the Kenoma, seeking Valentinus. Stumbling upon a height, he mounted it and observed a large force of foot soldiers marching east. Their banner was a cross, their armor blue and shining in the dull sun of Lucifer. Climbing down from the height, Perscors confronted a being masked as Olam, carrying a large red hammer. With both swords ready, Perscors cried out against the masked figure, who backed away, laughing and chanting:

"They go to massacre your Manichee friends, ill luck to both sides!

"Let the two serpents sting one another to death!

"Or go back if you will, in your darkness, and be cut down by either side!

"By the sons of Darkness calling themselves the Light, or the sons of the Light which is only another Darkness!"

Perscors charged at the masked taunter, both swords poised, but could not wholly dodge the hammer, which swung, huge and bloody, near his forehead. He woke this time shouting his defiance, crouched on his knees, a sword in each hand. But he ceased abruptly and sank his ear against the ground. The floor of the forest seemed to shake. Perscors rose, in the conviction that an enemy force was close by, marching toward the Manichees. However it came, the second dream was a call of warning, and his own outcry upon waking might have been heard. Whoever the approaching force might be, Perscors felt just enough sympathy for the Manichees to want to warn them.

Despite his efforts, it was well past dawn when he reached the boundary of the Manichee camp. On his march, he had discovered that his left cheek was bloody, and that his forehead was bruised. Escorted to Herakleides, he told enough of the second dream to convince the headman that an attack was indeed imminent.

"Do you come only to warn us or to fight with us against the Darkness that usurps the cross?"

"Precisely who is it that comes against you?" Perscors asked.

"These are the Marcionites, Knowing Ones who follow Marcion as we follow Mani. Our enemies always, and enemies to Olam also. Though what you are to Olam, your dream confuses utterly."

"But who is the aggressor?" Perscors asked. "Have you provoked this attack?"

"You know only the little of us that I have told you," Herakleides said heavily, "but even that should teach you that we fight only defensively. The World of Light loves only peace. We are a pitiful few on Lucifer. If you live to go into the West, you will be surrounded by many thousands of the Marcionites."

Perscors pondered his situation. He felt real though limited sympathy for the Manichees, and he knew nothing of the sect marching against them. He did not trust either of his dreams. His desire again was to find Valentinus, and the Marcionites lay between him and his one true friend on this star. Was this coming battle *his* battle?

He closed his eyes, hoping to hear a call. But he was alone.

"I am for the battle," he heard himself saying.

"Why?" Herakleides asked.

"I cannot know why. But I have been assaulted too often here, on this world. And in more than one realm. I will not wait to see if these cross-bearers will assault me also. I am for your battle, and when together we have beaten these off, then I will go west. If any man or demon or godling comes against me, henceforward, on this planet, he will learn that Primal Man is not always to be defeated."

CHAPTER **18**

The Manichees: Battle; Return of Nekbael

A T N O O N, the Marcionites attacked. Perscors had de-
clined both shield and javelins. He took up his stance in
the center of the first of the Manichees' three battle
lines. The two short swords he had brought back from
the netherworld now seemed to him extensions of his
own arms. Serenely self-possessed, he longed for the battle, *his* battle, rather than that of the Manichees.

The Marcionites came on in three lines also, but
Perscors estimated the lines to be much more fully
manned than the stretched-out ranks of the Manichees.
As the attack was launched, the Marcionites united in a
war cry, spurred on by trumpets and drums. Wave after
wave of javelins were hurled against the Manichee lines,
two falling just short of Perscors. Elated, Perscors did

not wait for the enemy to come up to him, but charged
alone into their midst. Within moments he had cut down
the three men in the Marcionite front line that he could
reach. His onslaught broke the second line and carried
him on against a circle of men from the third line that
formed around him. From then on, his battle proceeded
wholly independently of the larger conflict, which rapidly turned into a rout, with the Manichees fleeing. But
in the center the Marcionites became convinced that
they confronted a demon, not a man. Javelins and arrows
grazed Perscors, swords nicked him, but the dead piled
up so thickly that he stood at last bulwarked by a mound
of enemy corpses. The Marcionites fell back on all sides
of him, unwilling to press another assault, but equally
reluctant to permit the escape of so murderous a demon.

Rather than be a standing target for javelins and
arrows, Perscors unhesitatingly charged west against the
ring encircling him. The Marcionites broke before him;
their fear of demonic force overcame their desire to revenge the many men Perscors had hacked down. Instinc-
tively, he compelled himself to keep running until deep
in the woods, but the pursuit was ill-organized and dissolved rapidly, except for two warriors fiercer or more
courageous than the others. They maintained pace with
Perscors and kept him in sight. When he was deep
enough within the forest, Perscors swung around and
waited for them to come up to him. They loosed their
javelins almost simultaneously only a few yards away,
but by then Perscors had begun to charge again and
both lances passed harmlessly, one on each side of him
as he came forward. Perscors cried out his joy in the
strong pleasure of the double kill, as he chopped down
both men. Falling to his knees in exhaustion and in re-

lease of tension, he realized with a curious detachment that only the delight of slaughter was keeping him in some state of reality. Except when he killed, he seemed to be living in a vivid phantasmagoria. If the price of reality was to be the death of others, then he could not hope for indefinite survival on this religion-mad world to which he had voyaged.

After he had rested, he sensed some presence near him in the woods. With increasing dread, he looked up to the treetop level and saw there the phantasmal figure of Nekbael floating by very rapidly, her red hair streaming out in the wind. Perscors fought back against panic. To confront again that Medusa stare was beyond his strength. But he remembered the effect of the call. What if it did not come again? Was there only his own name to free him from her spell? What was in his name? The knowledge of what he had become. Had he any other knowledge? Of what he had been?

"In any case, I have not long to wait," he said aloud. Brooding on his dilemma, with the demonic danger ahead of him and human foes in his line of retreat, he resolved to go farther west, deeper into the forest. Somewhere up ahead, Nekbael doubtless awaited him in a meadow or clearing, but his heimarmene was there also, to the west, and he refused to identify Nekbael with his cosmic fate, however oppressive that might turn out to be.

It was late afternoon when he reached another clearing. The wind had been rising to gale force, but the meadow he entered was uncannily still. Nekbael was there, unveiled and unsmiling, but she turned away as he approached. With relief and some puzzlement, he took this for a sign that the ordeal of the earlier enchantment was not to be repeated. Was he to walk right by her? Her averted face gave him that choice. He hesitated and reflected on the three she-devils, if so they were, that he had encountered on Lucifer. Toward Achamoth, he felt fear and hatred and the wish for vengeance, but he sensed a more disturbing desire as well. Toward Ruha, her daughter, he felt both bewilderment and a positive passion, perhaps even an absurd hope of affection, but tempered by the horror that had overtaken his reflected self. The female in his presence moved him the most subtly, though the least inwardly of the three. She was, somehow, more his kind, less of an otherness. More swiftly than he could realize, he went up to her and gently turned her toward him, by a very slight touch upon her left shoulder. Their glances met, and this time he was not frozen in a spell.

"Shall we not at least speak?" Perscors murmured, his wariness overcome by his astonishment at her beauty when her face was turned fully upon him.

"Am I to tell you old stories?" she replied, with a dry bitterness.

"It is an oddity of this world I have come to that no one tells me more than a few shreds of a story. I would welcome a fuller account from anyone's lips."

He had spoken with ironic intent but felt no irony in the silence following, during which he found himself staring at her lips. They were the startling crimson of her hair. Though he understood that he was about to become her lover, a hesitancy began to gather in him again. Even if she intended no harm this time (which seemed unlikely), he was only a few hours' distance from the battlefield. If his enemies had decided to follow him, they could not be far away. Exhaustion, hunger, and thirst combined in him with the wish to embrace this dangerous glory that had come against him. But even as he encircled her waist and felt the fullness of her body's movement toward him, another awareness began in him. His palpable pleasure in battle was near-allied to his expectations of joy and pain at the hands of Nekbael.

She disrobed as he removed his armor. The windless meadow had become unnaturally bright and intensely hot. Nekbael lay on the grass, urgently beckoning Perscors down, but the heat was now so intolerable that he stumbled in his faintness as he endeavored to join her. Belatedly, he remembered the Manichean fivefold evil: smoke, fire, wind, water, darkness. As he entered Nekbael, a smoky fog settled over the meadow. Burning was everywhere, the wind suddenly rose, there was a sound of ocean water in his eardrums, and the brightness now blinded him. He could not see her face when he raised his head, but only a hazy glare that was a darkness to him. She pulled his head back to hers and bit through his lips, as her fingertips slashed his back like so many carving knives. Her hold was far stronger than his. He could not pull away or raise his head again or still the endless circular movements of their lovemaking. Perscors knew death to be very close by, as the orgasm continued unrelentingly. The pain in his lips and back became unbearable, and a still more terrible pain spread out from his loins. Nekbael's hands went from his back to his throat and started to strangle him. He lost his last sense of resistance and yielded to the overwhelmingly painful pleasure of what might be his end. Only a touch of chagrin, a hint of regret at an abandoned quest for knowing, hovered near him as he lost consciousness.

When the Marcionite search party found Perscors, he

lay naked, doubled up as though in pain, but he had struggled back near his swords and armor. They turned him over and discovered that he still lived. Bound, still naked, and barely conscious, he was carried westward into the country of the Marcionites. They did not notice the ring with a black gem that had been thrust into his left gauntlet, when they gathered that up for spoils together with the rest of his armor and the two short, thick swords. For some hours after they had left, a bright haze enveloped the meadow.

CHAPTER **19**

Olam on the Road West: The Pearl

F U R T H E R W E S T, Olam followed his path through
the lands of the Marcionites. One scouting party came
upon him, but retreated rapidly at the sight of the un-
gainly, yellow-complexioned, hulking figure.

"They've been warned," Olam grunted to himself as he
hastened on. He assumed that Perscors was a prisoner of
one people or another but dismissed the recognition as of
no importance. If Perscors did not return from Lucifer, it
would not be because of human violence, or so Olam
believed himself to know.

Forested mountain valleys had yielded to prairies,
with occasional clusters of hills. Passing through some
particularly high hills, Olam peered down into a sudden

valley and saw a solitary youth sitting by a fire. Olam
descended and sat by the fire, returning the smile of the
startled boy.

"Queer-looking creature you are, yellow man! *Are* you
a man, or something else?"

"Something else," Olam replied with high good
humor. He stared shrewdly at the young man. "Have you
a story to tell me?"

"Only my own story."

"I was in a great hurry"—Olam laughed—"but for
your story I have time enough. Let me hear it. I may
have a gift for you in return."

The youth stirred the fire and began to recite, in a
high, steady, cheerful voice, the happiest voice that
Olam had heard on Lucifer: "When I was only a small
child, living in the house of the king my father, rejoicing
in the splendor and wealth of those who educated me,
my parents sent me away from our home, the East, with
all I needed for my journey. Out of the wealth of our
treasure house, they tied together a burden for me,
weighty, yet light, so that I could carry it by myself.
Five kinds of precious substance they packed together:
gold, silver, chalcedony, agates, and diamonds. They
took off my robe of glory, which in their love they had
made for me, and removed my purple mantle, which was
measured out and woven to my proportions, and they
made a covenant with me and wrote it in my heart, beyond forgetfulness: 'Should you go down into the land
below us, and bring back the pearl now encircled by the
hissing serpent, from the midst of the sea, then you may
put on your robe of glory and your mantle over it, and
with your brother, next to us in rank, you shall become
heir to our kingdom.'

"Therefore I departed from the East, and went downward, accompanied by two guards, since the way was dangerous and I was too young for such a trip. I passed beyond the place where Eastern merchants gathered, until I reached the land of Babel and entered the walls of that great towered city. I went down then into the land below, and my companions abandoned me. Immediately I went to the serpent and took up my stance near his dwelling place, until he should drowse and fall asleep, so that I might take the pearl away from him.

"Because I was all alone, and a stranger to others in that place, I was glad when there I saw one of my own clan, a fair and handsome youth from the East, another son of kings. He came to me, and I made him my friend and the companion of my mission. Though he warned me of the people of that land below and against sharing with the Unclean, nevertheless I clothed myself in their robes, lest they suspect that I had come from outside to take the pearl and so awaken the serpent against me.

"Yet somehow they discovered that I was not of their country. With cunning they set a trap for me; I ate of their meat and I drank what they mixed for me. I served their king and forgot that I myself was the son of a king. I forgot the pearl for which my parents had sent me. Heavy with their food, I was thrown into a deep slumber.

"All this that I suffered my parents saw, and they grieved for me. There was a proclamation in their kingdom that all should come to their gates. And the kings and nobles and all the great ones of the East together devised a plan so that I would not be abandoned in the land below. They wrote a letter to me and each one signed it in his own name.

From your father, the King of Kings, and from your mother, possessor of the East, and from your brother, next to us in rank, to our son in the land below, our greeting. Awake, and rise up out of your sleep and recognize the words of our letter. Remember that you are a king's son; gaze upon that which you have served in your bondage. Remember the pearl, for whose sake you descended into the land below. Recall your robe of glory, remember your mantle of splendor, that you may put them on again and your name be read in the book of courage, and then you will be, together with your brother, heir to our kingdom.

"The king sealed the letter with his right hand against the children of Babel and against all the demons of tyranny. In the form of an eagle, king of all birds, the letter flew up and landed beside me and became speech entirely. At the sound of its voice I woke up, rose from my slumber, took it, kissed it with tenderness, broke its seal, and read. Just what was written in my heart was written in it. I remembered at once that I was the son of kings, and I longed for freedom. I remembered also the pearl for which I had been sent to the land below, and I began to charm the hissing and terrible serpent. I put it to sleep by naming to it the name of my father, the name of my brother and that of my mother, queen of the East. I took the pearl and turned back to the home of my father. I put off the filthy and impure garment and left it behind in the land below. Immediately I directed my way so that I might come to the light of my homeland, the East.

"On the way, I found the letter that had awakened me. Even as its sound had raised me up from slumber, so now its light shone from it and showed me the way.

With love drawing me on and guiding me, I steered past Babel on my left and reached my home country.

"My parents sent their treasurers to meet me, bearing my robe of glory and my mantle of splendor. I had forgotten my own brightness, for I had left it behind in my father's palace when I was still a young child. Suddenly I saw the mantle, and to me it seemed to become the mirror image of myself; I saw myself whole in it; that while the reflection and I were separate, yet our forms were the same. I saw also the treasurers who carried the mantle, that they were two, yet one form was present in each, one royal sign in both. The image of the King of Kings was shown throughout all the mantle.

"Also, I saw the movements of the Gnosis tremble all through the mantle. I saw that it was ready to speak. It said: 'I belong to him, most courageous of all men, whose acts have augmented my stature.' The impulses of the king stretched the mantle toward me, and my love aroused me to rush to meet the king and receive the mantle. I reached out and took it and decked myself with the beauty of all its colors.

"When I had put it on, I rose up to the gate of salutation and worship. I bowed my head, and I adored the radiance of my father, who had sent the mantle to me. I had fulfilled his instructions, and he had fulfilled his promises. He rejoiced over me and received me, and I was with him in his kingdom. All his servants praised him with pleasant voices, because he had promised I would journey to his court, and now my pearl and I indeed appeared before him."

Olam stared at the fire. Some of the bitterness had ebbed in him. He smiled and spoke in a voice so gentle that he hardly recognized it as being his own: "The gift

is to me. And the serpent, the sea, and the land below—
all are this cosmos. You wore their garment to deceive
the Archons, and yet the deception deceived you also."

"I heard the call of the letter," the youth said simply.

"You were both called and caller. We are as much a
deadly poison for the Darkness as the Darkness is for
us."

"They never told me the meaning of the pearl."

Olam stared at him for a long time.

"You do not need to be told. Your meaning and its
meaning are separate but the same."

The young man puzzled it out, as he looked at Olam,
who now would not avert his eyes from the fire.

"Then there was no quest," he said at last to Olam.

"There is always the quest. But you, subject and object of it, cannot know that you know."

"I did not suffer," the young man said.

"There need be no suffering, of one for another. That
is a great unwisdom. The combat is with ignorance and
not with sin."

Both sat silently.

"Were not the dangers real?" the youth broke silence
to ask.

"The dangers are there to be overcome. But the ordeal
is not the quest. That is the error of those who believe
and do not know, and of the Archons. And of the Primal
Man, each time he comes again."

Olam rose, gravely saluted the youth, and turned his
darkening path again to the West.

CHAPTER 20

The Marcionites: Captivity

CARRIED WEST by his captors, Perscors passed from his shocked semiconsciousness into the abysses of sleep. In a dream, he stood in the wastes of the Kenoma, watching Valentinus march by on the horizon, going west. He realized that Valentinus could not see him, and wondered if they would speak to one another ever again.

Olam marched up to him. It had begun to snow. Perscors stood directly in Olam's path and called out: "West is not the way! We are all deceived! All we oppose and what we seek are now in the North!"

Olam pushed him aside and marched westward.

"Olam!" Perscors called out, and was awake. He was dressed in green, in garments stripped from the corpse of some Manichee, and he shivered in a stone dungeon, his wrists chained to the wall.

The door to his cell was opened, and three guards armed with swords escorted in a tall, white-bearded figure of authority, magnificently attired, with a gold cross sewn on his white robe. Cerdo, bishop of the Marcionites, had come to view the captive Manichean demon.

He addressed Perscors skeptically but with a touch of respect: "Stranger, you look to me neither demon nor Manichean. You called out Olam's name? Are you a companion and follower of Olam?"

"I came to this world with him."

"Why did you fight against us? We have no love for Olam, but until now he has been at peace with us."

"I fought because you were many, and the Manichees were few. And you came against us. I fought in self-defense."

"So it was not at Olam's command?"

"He brought me here, but I am not his follower, or anyone's follower. What is Olam, anyway? Is he a man or something beyond?"

Cerdo studied his prisoner carefully. Rather doubtfully, he replied: "No, he cannot be a man. The Knowing Ones call him an Aeon. To us he seems something worse, though we are not certain. Better than a demon but not part of the glory of the Aeons."

Perscors shook his head in bafflement. Cerdo reflected for a while and then spoke slowly: "Whatever you are, you have killed many of ours and in a quarrel not your own. Is there some reason why we should spare you?"

Perscors was silent. His strength slowly was returning

to him, and with it came his confidence that this sect of warriors would not be the cause of his death.

"If you have nothing to say, then hear my judgment. I give you over to the ordeal of fire, after torture by the women of the fighters whom you killed. Justice is all you merit, and Olam cannot hold our justice against us."

Confronting Perscors's impassivity, Cerdo felt an ebb of his own confidence. This stranger, though a man, might be more than a man, without knowing it. Old prophecies might touch upon him, and truth might speak through him, though he himself embodied no truth. Uncertain and troubled, Cerdo resolved to contend for Perscors's soul, while consigning the stranger's body to the fire.

"What is your faith?" Cerdo asked.

Despite his situation and his slowly mounting fury, Perscors found himself laughing at the prospect of explaining his dried-up American Presbyterianism to a belated representative of second-century heresy. The madness of phantasmagoria was coming upon him again, and with it the need to kill or be killed. But he had cunning enough to suppress his hysterical laughter.

"I believe nothing, except that I am here to some purpose. I will not perish by your fire or any fire but my own, and those who seek to murder me will suffer for it."

Cerdo tried to summon anger, but felt only dread. "Who sent you to be a scourge unto this world?"

"I came of my own will, seeking my own freedom."

"Freedom," Cerdo said severely, "is only of the will of the Father."

"There is no freedom on Lucifer or on earth," Perscors

replied, "except knowing your own fate and either coming to love it or fighting against it."

"Hear the gospel of Marcion," Cerdo cried out, and his voice began to take on authority. "There is nothing worth saying about Beginnings, and neither you nor these Knowers have any knowledge worth the having. Redemption is by faith, faith in the unknown God who is not of this world. Those who proclaim the Gnosis are in the right only about *this* world. God did not make it, and his Son cannot save it. Olam knows correctly that the good God is an alien god. What he does not understand is that we always were, we are, and we must remain strangers to the true God. Until we are saved, we wholly belong to our maker, the Demiurge."

"From what are you saved, then? Why should the true God save you if you are not his?"

Cerdo answered unhesitatingly: "We are saved from our creator, to be adopted by the new and alien God, who reaches out to us because of his goodness, though we are not his."

"What difference does that make to this world?" Perscors asked slowly.

"This world cannot be bettered. Neither our nature, nor the world's nature, can be altered. These puny elements, this miserable cell of the Demiurge, deserve only the rule of justice. The good God does not deign to touch this world."

"I hardly see why you and the Manichees should be at war," Perscors observed. "They brood on Beginnings and say they are transformed by knowing God, but they despair of this world as much as you do. And at least they are less bloodthirsty in their justice than you are."

"We vex the Demiurge," Cerdo insisted gruffly. "But the Manichees do his work for him."

Perscors shook his head. "I find no truth in what you say. Whatever the confusions of the Manichees, they tell a story of a Primal Man that explains what is strongest in me."

Cerdo sighed in anger. "You are of the Demiurge, and justice condemns you. In an hour, you go to the revenge of our women and then to the fire."

Left alone by Cerdo and the guards, Perscors considered his predicament. It would be unwise to wait, though his fullest strength had not yet returned. The daemon in him said: "Now." He gathered his force, and pulled easily away from the wall. Until he recovered the armor and swords of Siniavis, his chains must be his weapons, as they had been against the women of Achamoth.

He went up to the cell's door, dashed a chain against it, and then stood aside to the left of the door. It swung open and two guards ran in. Perscors crushed the face of the second with one sweep of his chained wrist and turned on the other, who collapsed onto the cell's floor in terror. One impulse in Perscors told him to turn away, but rage dominated and he smashed in the cowering figure's skull with another blow. Only then did he turn and march out of the cell of his captivity.

It was near dawn as he emerged into the central compound of the Marcionites. Though he seemed unobserved and felt confident he could break through whatever sentries were stationed at the western border of the Marcionites, he had no intention of departing without his armor and swords. In the lightening darkness he made his wandering way through the stone labyrinths of the Marcionite center, which seemed half town and half encampment. There were lights in just a few of the rude stone houses, most of which were oblong, barrack-like structures. Only once did he meet a sentry, whom he strangled from behind, swiftly and noiselessly. The chain had already fallen off his left wrist, and now he found his right wrist free also. He shrugged off the loss of the chains and walked west steadily through his enemies' dwelling place.

A bleak dawn came. Perscors had reached the western precincts and realized he could not linger. The ground began to slope downward, and ahead was a heavily wooded valley. In the distance, Perscors saw a four-man patrol, which was moving away from him. Bitter at the loss of armor and swords, he suppressed his rage and hastened down the slope into the valley.

CHAPTER 21

Escape to Vision

P E R S C O R S   L A Y in ambush in the woods, secure in the anticipation that a patrol would pass. He had ceased to question the daemonic inwardness that had taken possession of him. A plan seemed unnecessary; when the patrol came, he would know what to do.

A single Marcionite came down the forest trail, armed with a javelin and carrying a leather pouch containing what Perscors assumed were provisions. Whether the rest of the patrol were close behind did not concern him. As the Marcionite passed in front of him, Perscors rose and rushed at the man. A single strangled cry and the unequal struggle ended. Armed with the javelin, Perscors ran back on the path, seeking other victims, but the patrol fled before him, to seek reinforcements. Reluctantly, he turned back and retrieved the pouch, which contained a round, flat loaf of bread and a flask of water. Refreshed, he continued westward through the woods, though troubled now by recollections of his dream of the Kenoma.

Noon came, and he was still deep in the woods. But he began to be aware that the forest was changing. Mist rose everywhere and gradually became so thick that he could see only a few feet in front of him. Was it still a forest? The ground became damper and a rising wind blew against him. Somewhere up ahead there clashed a sound of waters, and Perscors felt the sense of reality ebbing in him. A third encounter with Nekbael might be imminent, and he vowed to avoid such agony if he could.

His pace slowed as the noise of breaking water came closer. Surely there was no ocean ahead, so that what he heard had to be illusion. He moved now through land closer to wilderness marsh than to forest. If he approached another ordeal, then he associated the trial with Nekbael. But suddenly he ceased to expect torment.

A single leaf that he had focused upon had changed from green to the silver color of shining water. Refocusing followed, and now everything he could see was silvery water.

Perscors felt himself ascending even as he *saw* himself descending to the glory of the water. He gripped the javelin tighter, as a defense not against any anticipated enemy but against what must be a vision.

He stood surrounded by the shining. So great was the glare that for relief he gazed at his own feet and saw only the glitter of marble. But when he prodded the marble with his javelin, he stirred up shining water.

"What is the meaning of these waters?"

Perscors had shouted the question aloud. He was answered by a hail of stones, coming at him from all sides. To protect himself, he dropped the javelin and crouched over, placing his head between his knees. He did not feel any stones striking.

He found himself saying a name he had not heard before: Ialdabaoth. How many times he repeated the name he could not know, for in his kneeling position he had passed into a trance-like state. Visions came by him which were not dreams, as he stayed awake, head pressed tight against himself. But the visions, though distinct, were too rapid to afford him more than glimpses. Enormous marble halls, one after another, came by him, or was it that he went from one to another? Each chamber initially seemed endless, with ceilings as high as the heavens, yet each yielded to another. And all were empty. They were bare of everything except the splendor of their own marble.

At the end of the visions he saw fire on every side of him. Yet this seemed his own fire, and he remained cold, chilled through.

Perscors came out of the visions and rose, stiff from his long crouching. The javelin lay on the dry floor of the forest. He could hear a wind moving upon him from the north, but no sound of water. After a while, he picked up his javelin and resumed his westward march.

CHAPTER **22**

Saklas in Siniavis

B E L O W , I N Siniavis, Saklas the Demiurge tried to re-
joice in his apotheosis. He stood in the great central hall
of his temple, before his own image, and accepted the
homage of his worshippers.

The Saklaseum, towering above Siniavis upon a foun-
dation a hundred steps high, was a gigantic domed
structure surrounded on all four sides by chambers,
stairs, and secret corridors, and above by quarters for the
priests and cells for sacrificial victims. An open court
surrounded the building, and about this ran four porti-
cos. Gold and ivory were dominant in the façade of the
structure.

So colossal were the proportions of Saklas's statue that
its outstretched hands touched either wall of the central

hall. It was fashioned of gold and ivory over a wooden core, which was sacred. The walls of the temple were plated with bronze, with a second inner plating of silver, and an innermost plating of gold. The entire great chamber was windowless but was lit by a luminosity radiating from Saklas himself.

Amid the fervor of his devotees, and despite his customary sense of exaltation, the Demiurge felt an uncertainty and even an anxiety spreading both in them and within himself. The Aeon Olam marched west on Lucifer, and probably no force could suffice to restrain him. Only deception, which kept Olam moving in the wrong direction, seemed available to Saklas.

He needed allies, he reflected, even as he acknowledged the uneasy raptures of his subjects. Too much enmity at once was loose upon his world: Olam; the obsessed heresiarch, Valentinus, who would be dangerous when memory was wholly restored to him; Perscors, a violent form of the Anthropos, of pre-existent man, now returned inopportunely. The thoughts of Saklas turned to his terrible mother: Achamoth. She was the most ambivalent of allies, but against three such adversaries he required a formidable force if his laws were to prevail.

His ceremony over, his followers withdrawn, he lapsed into reverie. There was always a confusion in his mind when he contemplated the Beginnings. His earliest memory was of seeing himself reflected in a glassy ocean. He had reached forth into the waters to embrace himself, and had entered a whirlpool, from which his mother had rescued him. He could recall precisely the shock of being plucked out by her and his wild grief at abandoning the embrace of his own shadow.

The trace of confused dread seemed always to be gaining in him. He had spirited away Olam's tower, in the absence of that Aeon, and had concealed it in his own secret place. For how many ages he had struggled to make this world, only to see it threatened each time his ugly, yellow-hued enemy returned! The curse of his own powerlessness lingered during Olam's absences and became a humiliation beyond endurance whenever Olam quested again for the ruin the Aeons miscalled "freedom."

He would go up and into the waste places of Lucifer, Saklas suddenly decided. There, in the Kenoma, Olam, Valentinus, and Perscors each marched west, in the land without a people, between the Marcionites and the Arimaneans. And there, in the waters of Night, let them drown or be swept to the farthest west, where no life was, or could be. But he would need help, Saklas realized again. His strength was of his mother, and to her, despite his dread, he must turn.

Saklas emerged from below at dawn in a green valley, only a short space from the Temple of Ennoia. He came up in the person of a priest of Ennoia and waited beneath a plane tree for whichever of his adversaries first arrived. But he waited in the cunning of desperation, heartsick at his own waning strength and in growing terror at the advent of Achamoth.

CHAPTER **23**

Valentinus at the Temple of Ennoia

A N H O U R after dawn, Valentinus stood in front of the Temple of Ennoia.

Except for one priest who sat smiling under a plane tree, the temple's front seemed deserted. Valentinus hesitated for a few moments, suffering from an indistinct return of many memories.

The temple had a single, small blue dome, set over an undistinguished boxlike structure, which was stark white. But the six steps leading up to the entrance were blood red. He took the steps in rapid stride, but on the sixth he stopped and did not go through the temple door, which he could see was ajar. Perhaps returning memory alone might have stopped him, but at his feet on the sixth step was a gold inscription: TO SIMON THE POWER

OF GOD WHICH IS CALLED GREAT. As he read the inscription, Valentinus recalled the story of Simon the Mage, and remembered that Simon's whore Helena had been called his Ennoia, the Thought of God fallen into exile— his Sophia-Prunikos. Was he recalling what he had read, Valentinus wondered, or was the knowledge based on experience? And how did he know that this was Ennoia's temple?

He pushed the door open and went in. The bare temple consisted of a stone floor, stone sides, the dome above, and nothing more. Valentinus gazed up at the dome. There was a menace conveyed by it, but too obscurely for Valentinus to be able to interpret the danger. He turned, went out and down the six stairs. The priest was gone from under the plane tree.

Valentinus sat in the tree's shade. He knew better than to strive to remember. For the first time on Lucifer, he felt the imminence of full recall.

The shade darkened. He saw himself within, below the dome, yet knew it was not his temple. Robed men and women sat before him, on marble benches, Perhaps they were forty in number. They were not his disciples but of an earlier teaching, which he had come to fulfill. Though they listened gravely to his homily, they gave no signs either of agreement or of dissent. Gradually Valentinus became aware that he could *see* into the past, but that he could not *hear* what he himself was saying. He strained to hear, despite his realization that he would not hear unless he ceased the attempt.

A clatter of voices rose around him, challenging, threatening, denouncing. But within this outer rim of tumult he began to hear his own voice, addressing the congregation in the temple. An armed band of Marcionites had surrounded the plane tree, but they fell silent when Valentinus spoke to the congregants of his vision:

"From the beginning you are immortal and children of life eternal. It was your wish to take death as your portion to yourselves, that you might destroy death, that you annihilate it utterly, so that death might die in you and through you. For when you destroy the world and yourselves are not destroyed, then you are lords over the whole creation, then you are lords over all decay."

The congregation faded before Valentinus. He looked up at what should have been blue sky beyond the plane tree, but saw the blue dome and realized that he was within the temple. It was no longer bare, though he was alone. Whether he was in an earlier time or not, he no longer knew or cared. Nor did he care about the patrol, which must be startled and bewildered by his vanishing, and which might enter the temple, if it dared and if its time was one with his time. But he doubted this, as he stared at the murals on the temple walls. Great serpents swam and danced before him on the murals. "Ophites," he said, and sat down on a marble bench to study them. They were not murals but screens, and upon them living pictures played, dissolving and flickering, reminding Valentinus of the doctrine that had preceded him and that he had revised into his truth.

The Archon Ialdabaoth took Adam, soon after the Archons had created him, and placed him in a paradise, that he might forget the pre-existent Adam, the Primal Man, by delighting in the deceptions of the Archons' world. Ialdabaoth thickened the eyes of Adam, that he might fail to gain knowledge through them.

But Ennoia, the lost thought of God, mother of the

Demiurge Ialdabaoth,—and by her other name, Achamoth, mother of Saklas—sent the serpent, that Adam
and Eve might defy Ialdabaoth and taste the fruit of
knowledge. So the Gnosis began, when Adam and Eve
had eaten and knew the power from beyond and turned
away from their makers, the Archons.

Valentinus glanced at the serpent writhing beneath
the Tree of Knowledge. This was the mystery of Eden;
this was the serpentine river of life that flowed out of the
paradise that was prison. And at last Valentinus recognized the words of his own evangel returning to him:

"Olam became a fruit of the knowledge of the Father.
He did not, however, destroy those who ate of it. He
rather caused them to be joyful because of this dis-
covery."

He had been brought to Lucifer, Valentinus now
understood, to find again the place of the Pleroma, the
place of rest, which did not belong to the Archons. Resolving to quest on toward the place, he turned away
from the murals to the door. An impulse caused him to
turn around again. The temple again was bare and
ruined, the murals gone. Before Valentinus could turn
again, the door swung open and the smiling priest of
Ennoia entered quietly, with a finger to his lips, warning
Valentinus to be silent. Still smiling, he indicated with
nods of his head the continued danger of the patrol outside the temple.

Valentinus stared at the priest, but waited for
guidance. Taking Valentinus by the arm, the priest of
Ennoia led him behind the ruined altar, where stairs led
downward. A tunnel, Valentinus guessed, as without
emotion he followed the priest, who was Saklas, downward and into labyrinthine turnings.

CHAPTER **24**

Ruha: Escape to the Sea

F A R T H E R   W E S T, Perscors lay on the floor of the
forest, ear pressed against the ground, listening. He
sensed a danger ahead, and yearned to hear some presage, but none came. Sleep, fought off for a time, overwhelmed him.

In dream, a figure of light appeared before him, stepping into the filthy mud, stepping into the clouded
water. Bending over Perscors, he implored anxiously:
"Since you are a Son of the Great, why has your living
fire become transformed?"

"Ruha," Perscors answered, and in answering he was
awake. She must be ahead somewhere; and in serenity
he prepared his spirit for whatever ordeal might come.

He knew now that west, for him, was only more painful pleasure and pleasurable pain. Why he had the vision that the Pleroma, lost tower and place of rest, truly lay north, he could not know, yet the vision was his and was not open to Olam and Valentinus.

Though he alone knew that west was a deception, he would keep on: to meet Valentinus a last time, if he could, but also to confront and overcome his own fate. If he survived to go north, then it would be well; if not, then not. Returning to earth held no interest for him.

The daemonic women were involved in his fate: Ruha, Achamoth, Nekbael. He had a dim foreboding that there yet might be a fourth. Rising, he started west again in the forest.

Perscors did not go far. One thicket ahead, Ruha waited for him. He experienced neither rancor nor fear when he saw her again. Some part of him mused on the detachment that seemed so total in him. To feel consciously neither curiosity nor desire ought to have bewildered him, but acceptance of what might come dominated instead. Or was it that his calm protected him from understanding the nature of his desires?

Their reunion began as an idyll, played against a gentle clearing. When he emerged into the cool green light, Ruha sat only a few yards away, on a great black stone covered with moss. A stream ran nearby through the meadow, ringing out four notes, each higher than the last. Ruha was clad in a loose white robe gathered at her wrists and throat. Her feet were bare. Her black hair hung loose and was draped over her knees. Expressionless, her huge black eyes stared through Perscors, not as though he was absent, but as though his presence was a momentary accident.

"To her I am an instrument, to be used, to be broken," Perscors told himself as he came up to Ruha. He touched her forehead with his left hand, holding on to the javelin with his right. Still looking through him, she brushed his hand away and rose up, saying: "Not here," in a commanding voice. She walked along the stream, for only a few steps, and abruptly she vanished. Following her, Perscors stepped onto the place of her disappearance, and at once found himself in another place, alone in a vast hollow cavern, pleasantly soft and dark. He rounded a single turning and found her waiting for him in a half-lit chamber of black stone. At its farther end was the entrance to another chamber, still more dimly lit.

Ruha stood expectantly, her elbows drawn back, her eyes narrowed. Mounting desire was tempered by wariness in Perscors. The chamber disturbed him because of a sense that he had been there before, though he had not, and also because of his awareness that it was only a prelude to the chamber beyond, of which he felt an obscure dread.

"Are we alone here? Or do you have others nearby, ready to surprise me?"

She did not answer, her stance and smile remaining the same. Perscors did not believe that she was alone, but doubted also that there was anyone in the next chamber. Yet he continued to hesitate, while alternately studying her face and the room. He recalled in her features no actual persons whom he had seen, even in his childhood, but rather visions of a possible woman that had haunted him as far back as memory could go. The room, decorated in white and scarlet furs, and empty except for a large wide couch, could not be identified with either his fantasies or his experience and yet was intensely familiar.

"How deep down are we? Surely not back in Siniavis, where you play murderous games with drugged, crazed doubles?"

She would not answer but continued to watch him with narrowed eyes, as though waiting for some break in his will that she knew must come. Without warning, he turned around and went back into the dark hollowness of the great cavern. "Let her come after *me* if she wants me," he said to himself, and he determined to find his way back to the clearing above. But the cavern became totally dark, and he had no choice but to wander back to her chamber.

It was the same, except that she was gone. Again he had no choice but to attempt the farther chamber. Here he found her, crouched in a corner, the pupils of her eyes now much wider as they focused upon him. Though she was alone in the room, he was oppressed by dread. As his eyes grew accustomed to the quarter light, he saw that they were in a torture chamber, with whipping posts and a long, low table embellished with chains fastened to each corner. A few feet above the head of the crouching Ruha was a rude shelf piled with an array of whips and clubs.

They stared at one another. Perscors realized that she would not resist him. He had been led here to punish and to possess her in that punishment. What ritual was involved he could not know, and yet he suspected that the ritual purpose was to implicate him in some further act of self-destruction, a completion of the fate met by his mirror image in Siniavis. A lust to torment her, to make her scream, rose up in him, to be answered by a stronger impulse to protect whatever of his soul was left after the destruction of his shadow self in the underworld.

He turned, rushed out of the room, and ran back through the next chamber into the darkness of the cavern. It was better to be lost in a labyrinth than to be guided out by the demoness after he had scourged her and so yielded. In his rage against desire he hoped for battle again, and as he went forward in the darkness, he had an intimation that some combat awaited him. How long and far he ran he could not tell, since the vision of Ruha crouching expectantly did not leave him. After a time he saw light ahead and slowed his advance toward it. The cavern opened out on cliffs facing a raging sea. Blinded momentarily by the full light, Perscors gaped at an ocean wilder than any he had known.

CHAPTER **25**

Return of Achamoth

PERSCORS STOOD on a cliff of some seventy feet above the eddying of the sea. The cliff's point was marked with a square black stone. Evening approached, and in the light of the setting sun Perscors made out a kind of stair cut in the side of the cliff. Though the steps led nowhere except straight down into the sea and the light would soon fail, he resolved to go down.

His descent was rapid, and ended in a surprise. The ocean, which from above had been seen as washing the face of the cliff, appeared now to have ebbed far out. Between the waves and the cliff a quarter mile of black sand had been left bare. Rocks of the same color rose out of this bareness at intervals. Directly up against the cliff was a black altar. Halfway between the altar and the sea, a tall woman leaned against a rock, bathed in the glow of the setting sun. Perscors went toward her at a steady pace, until he recognized her and stopped, just out of range of a javelin throw.

Achamoth, robed in black fur, scowled at him in recognition. He went forward again and stopped only a few yards away, javelin at the ready.

"You are in Manichean garb this time, and armed! Your life remains forfeit to me, but the time is not yet."

Perscors weighed an attack. Could this being be slain or at least wounded? What stopped him was the necessity of grappling with her, if the javelin proved insufficient. The fear was of himself, whether in regard to mother or to daughter. He longed too greatly to humiliate, to lacerate, to enter Achamoth.

"A truce, for now, suits me also. But I offer an agreement. Wherever we are, I need to get back to the forest above. Guide me there. If not, I have no other way but to go up the cliff, find your daughter's cavern again, and compel her to take me to my path."

He waited, watching Achamoth's face and tightening his grip on the javelin. Fury came and went in her features, to be replaced by a bitter smile.

"You want her, and precisely as she wills to be wanted. But you wish to keep what you can of your soul. Keep it, for now!"

"Will you guide me back?"

"Yes, but by my way. It will not be a straight road."

He stood, pondering his choice. Whatever the turnings ahead, she had pledged his return. Better to follow her than to seek out Ruha again. The memory of Ruha's eyes, the pupils distended as she crouched, troubled him now. He studied the large eyes of Achamoth, as colorless as her daughter's were black.

"By what road do we go back?"

"I have a journey to make tonight. If you accompany me, then I will place you in your forest at dawn."

Perscors let the javelin fall, as a sign. She beckoned him to pick it up.

"I do not take you under my protection. We will be neither enemies nor friends through this night."

"I need no protection."

He retrieved the javelin and waited to follow her back to the stairs. But she turned around to the sea.

"I have no talent for walking upon water," Perscors said.

Achamoth turned to him again. "We are going on a voyage to an island. There is a boat concealed at the water's edge."

"What is on the island?"

"Memories."

With that word, she swung around decisively and strode down to the sea. Perscors followed, his steps more uncertain, as the darkness was now dense. Beyond the final and largest rock, they found a small sailboat. There was little wind, but Achamoth's will sufficed to drive the boat along at what seemed to Perscors an incredible swiftness.

He lost any grasp of time. The voyage was rough, and he brooded on the waves, feeling at one with them. Achamoth, had he noticed her, would have astonished him. Her brutal, angry pride left her. Grief, fear, bewilderment, and an expression of yearning ignorance replaced pride. But these metamorphoses of her features had nothing to do with the sea that beat so strongly against her onrushing boat.

They landed with a jolt, the boat suddenly running aground. Perscors, without reflection, leaped out, as though he were invading the island. Achamoth sat upright in the boat, as though not understanding that the voyage was over. Watching her, Perscors became aware that she had changed, that indeed she looked demoralized.

Perplexed, he waited for her, conscious that he was dependent upon a being who had lost all force and all apparent purpose. Anger rising, he resolved to stir her: "Achamoth! Rouse yourself!"

Like a sleepwalker she rose stiffly and stepped onto the land.

"Since we are here, what do we go to see or encounter in this moonless darkness?"

She did not seem to understand his question. Her stare was meaningless, without focus. Perscors shook her shoulder. When there was no reaction, he realized how absurd a dilemma now existed. His guide needed guidance, and he was totally lost.

He led her to a slight rise in the ground, and sat her down upon moss. What seemed her trance continued. He doubted that dawn would see him back upon his western path in the forest as she had promised. Weary and confused, he sat near her, looking with wonderment at her blank features. His horror and hatred of her had gone. Sympathy with so occult a being was grotesque, he thought, but he felt it nevertheless.

Abruptly she spoke into the darkness: "I was cast out into the Places of Shadow and of Emptiness. I found myself outside of the Light, and I looked at myself. I was as formless and as shapeless as an abortion, because I had conceived nothing.

"The Limit shaped me, but gave me no knowledge. I longed for the Light, but was held back by the Limit. I remained outside, in loneliness and abandonment.

"I mourned, because I had not conceived. I was in fear, lest life abandon me, as the Light had gone from me. My grief and consternation produced the substance from which the Demiurge made the cosmos.

"Saklas believed that he made all things by himself, but in reality he made them under my influence. He created a heaven without knowing heaven. He formed a man and did not know man. He produced an earth, without knowing earth. He knew nothing at all of the ideas of the things that he made, or of the mother.

"He thought that he was the only God, and said, through his prophets: 'Remember the former things of old: for I am God, and there is none else; I am God, and there is none like me.' "

In the ensuing silence, Perscors marveled that she had spoken with a voice not her own. Instead of her harsh, deep imperiousness, he had heard a voice that blended those of a feeble old woman and a small, lost girl. But her memories did not aid Perscors in finding his way back. How to deliver her from the trance mystified him. She had come to this island, it must hold something she needed to find or to recall. He resolved to leave her for now and to make his own search of the island, despite the darkness. His fortune, which had carried him through so much on this world, would bring him success again.

He had not gone far in the dark before he seemed to

have lost his javelin. Had he lost it? Or had an unseen branch taken it out of his hand? He went a little farther on, and halted abruptly.

What seemed alternately a snake and a lion flashed directly ahead of him, its eyes streaming fire. Weaponless, Perscors hesitated. But his own fire urged him onward. When he was close enough to the beast, he threw himself forward with the agility and force that had been increasing continually since his arrival upon Lucifer. To his fury, the serpentine lion twisted to the side, uttered a hissing roar, and ran away from him, with a speed he could not match. Just for a moment, as it evaded him, the beast's features had been clear to him. It had the face of a man, a face he remembered from Siniavis: Saklas the Demiurge. Dazed, Perscors turned back to find Achamoth.

She sat where he had left her; yet he saw as he came near that she had returned to herself.

"Do you know where you are, Achamoth?"

"I know. It is enough. I will stay for a time, but you need not wait until dawn. I will guide you to a place *here*, and it will become the place *there*."

"But what are you to Saklas? If that queer beast I frightened off *was* Saklas."

"Saklas as he was. Not now. I bore him here, as my child."

There was a desolation in her voice, but her expression was the prideful scowl he had seen before.

"Guide me to the place, then."

She rose and walked only seven steps. He followed close upon her in the darkness. Suddenly he stood in daylight, by the stream of his encounter with Ruha. He looked about the clearing and saw that he was alone.

Then he went out of the clearing toward the West. "I will encounter them all again—Ruha, Achamoth, Saklas," he said to himself, and added aloud: "Let them beware of me."

CHAPTER **26**

Desert and Deluge

OLAM ASSUMED that he was now much farther
west than Valentinus and Perscors could be. This intuition did not disturb him, but he was troubled nevertheless, and as he studied the landscape, he began to
understand the causes of his uneasiness.

He had come to the end of the Marcionite lands. Before him the Kenoma began, and beyond this muddy
world ought to be the region of the devil-worshipping
Arimaneans. There, amid horrors, Saklas had concealed
the one place on Lucifer that was no part of his creation,
the tower that Olam had built with his own hands, to
mark the place of the Pleroma. And there, Olam resolved, Valentinus would be healed and renewed. Per-

haps, he thought more dubiously, Perscors might win a release also, if he survived to get there.

But the muddy wastes of the Kenoma, as Olam now saw, extended only a short way from the high ground upon which he stood. Within sight, the wet waste places had dried up and desert spanned the whole horizon. Only the Demiurge could have reduced part of the Kenoma into desert. Olam was too subtle to interpret this imposition of desert as a barrier. More likely, it was a trap.

As he entered the new region, Olam was surprised at how cold it was. He would have expected a western desert on Lucifer to be warm. In this hostile territory, he ought to meet neither men nor animals. Unless, he grinningly reflected, Saklas had thrown in an oasis or two.

Some hours later he did come upon an oasis, and grew suspicious as he studied its elaborate but abandoned gardens, its overblown roses and extraordinarily vivid trees. He sat for an hour in a grove of plane trees, puzzled as to Saklas's tactics.

Olam knew that he was waiting for someone; it might be some messenger sent by Saklas. Ought he to wait? At the point of rising to depart, he heard the howl of jackals.

Suddenly they milled about him; their gold eyes glared, but their supple bodies twisted in terror of the Aeon. One jackal, bolder than the others, pressed against Olam, not in menace, but as though, in that cold desert, it needed the Aeon's warmth.

"They fear me," Olam mused, "but they fear what is coming even more."

He studied the jackal's eyes and then closed his own. Immediately he saw ocean, an ocean in tumult, with enormous waves rolling in just under the level of the sky.

Olam opened his eyes and looked up at the sky. Black clouds swayed heavily, from horizon to zenith. Abruptly he foresaw the danger: desert, and then deluge. Ancient visions crowded his inner sight. And an old text of the Knowers returned to him:

"For first there will come downpours of rain from the Demiurge, that Saklas might destroy all flesh if need be, but mostly those who derive from the seed of those into whom knowledge had penetrated. For those are strangers to Saklas. And unless a glory of the Aeons comes to them, they will perish in the waters."

"Unless an Aeon perishes in the waters also," Olam muttered. The dull gold of the jackal's eyes brimmed. Olam shook himself and stood up. Above, the whole dome of the sky had turned opaque with darkness. More of the text came back to Olam:

"Then the God of the Aeons will give to them of those who serve him, in that they follow the fiery burden.

"They will come to that land where the great men have come.

"Then will fire, brimstone, and asphalt be cast upon those men, and fire and darkness will come upon the Aeons, and the eyes of the powers of the Illuminators will become dark.

"And the Aeons will not see the Illuminators in those days."

Olam looked out to the western horizon. Against the descending blackness, he saw a glitter of silvery light.

The jackals bolted to the east. Olam swiftly began to tear down plane trees. Lashing them together, after they were stripped, he stood naked in the gathering storm.

His torn skin-and-leather garments had provided the lashings, plaited together with thick-clustered vines from the oasis.

As the silvery flood roared in, Olam mounted his raft.

CHAPTER **27**

The Waters of Night

V A L E N T I N U S   S A T   in a stone chamber, watching the priest of Ennoia perform a ritual.

The priest stood before a statue of a sea serpent and muttered names. Though the figure had been the size of a man, it seemed much smaller to Valentinus each time he looked at it. When he gazed again, after staring at the image of a deluge on the chamber's ceiling, he had to peer closely to see the statue at all.

Then he understood. When this image had shrunk away, a flood would gather in the world above. Suddenly Valentinus called aloud, without rising from his stone bench:

"You are no priest, but the Demiurge! Ialdabaoth, as

once I knew you upon earth, but here on Lucifer named Saklas."

"Memory floods you, heresiarch. I do not resent your interruption, since my task is accomplished. By now, Olam's wickedness is fated to be washed away into the Kenoma. Even an Aeon cannot swim for six days and six nights."

Valentinus stared scornfully at Saklas. After an interval, he spoke very quietly, but with the urgency of memory released after long oblivion:

"You are a great repeater of floods, always to small purpose. There is a story told of the Archons.

"They took counsel with each other, and said:

" 'Come let us make a deluge with our hands and destroy all flesh, men and beasts.'

"But you, the Ruler of the Archons, came to know of their decision, and you said to one man:

" 'Take of the wood that does not rot and hide in it, you and your children and the beasts and the birds.

" 'And set it upon my holy mountain.'

"Then Norea, a daughter of Knowledge, came to the man, wishing to board the hiding place of wood.

"And when he would not let her, she blew upon the wooden boat, and three times destroyed it.

"And boarded a fourth time, with Seth, Adam's son, and rode out the Archons' flood."

Saklas stood a long time, frowning upon Valentinus, who remained seated. Then the Demiurge spoke:

"Find your own way back to the world above, and your own way out of the waters.

"It is not given to me to punish you.

"Who can punish you? Who can know if you are alive?

"My faith is in the waters of night. Let them be a

judgment upon you, if there can be a judgment upon you.

"Let them judge Olam, and take him from me.

"Let them take the crazed giant, the Primal Man you have brought upon me."

Valentinus did not see Saklas vanish. Suddenly he was alone in the stone chamber. He rose and walked to the figure of the sea serpent. It was no more than four inches high.

Valentinus grasped the figure with his left hand.

He could not move it. The weight was absolute.

As he watched, it grew smaller before him.

When it was no more than two inches high, Valentinus grasped it with his right hand and raised it from the altar.

It was no lighter, but a strength more than his own was in Valentinus.

He crashed his hand, with the tiny serpent, against the altar. Pain flooded him. Both his hand and the serpent were broken. He swept the fragments of the serpent from the altar, with a single movement.

Holding his shattered hand before him, Valentinus began to mount the stairway out of the altar chamber. His one thought was to find Saklas, and to wound the Demiurge, even if he could not hope to destroy him.

As he climbed up, the pain in his hand increased. So did the realization that he had suffered precisely this pain before. He felt no fear for Olam, for Perscors, or for himself, but knew only the strong need to set himself against the flood of the Archons.

CHAPTER 28

The Hunter Nimrud

PERSCORS WOKE to the sound of rushing waters. The stream, near which he had slept, had become a raging river, with waves like an ocean's.

Rain began to fall, steadily but not alarmingly. After brooding on the transformation of the stream, Perscors looked behind him to the east, where the sky was a threatening black.

He remembered two texts: "My Spirit shall not always strive with man" and "It repenteth me that I have made them."

"What giant is there in this earth of Lucifer in these days?" Perscors asked aloud. The answer: it could be only himself. If the Archons and the warriors of this cosmos could not stop him, and they could not, then they would seek to drown him.

He looked up coldly at the eastern sky, and saw that its darkness was spreading quickly. He had not much time. But the fire that had carried him through would not be quenched by these waters. He felt a detached curiosity as to how, but not as to whether, he would survive.

"I will ride it out, but in what?"

Perscors walked west slowly, following the river. The rain fell more heavily. As the river widened, it seemed more and more an ocean, and took over nearly half the western horizon.

Intuiting an approach, Perscors turned around to the east. A clumsy old bark, seemingly deserted, drifted rapidly toward him. Very broad and low, filthy with bilge, yellow-sided, it had a badly split mainmast. The sails seemed crumpled, yet held up strongly in the wind.

Taking it as the sign of his ongoing fate, Perscors leaped aboard midship as it came by him.

At his feet lay a man, taller and broader even than himself. An icy wind had come up, and Perscors shivered violently as he stared at the matted-haired man, laid out in what seemed a shroud, yet staring back at him out of gray-green eyes still alive with anguish. Perscors knelt down near the man and placed his hand on his brow. The giant closed his eyes, but said to Perscors: "Who are you?"

"A wanderer from another cosmos. And you?"

Opening his eyes, the giant replied: "Nimrud the Hunter. This is my death ship. I sail back to the Arimaneans, in the West, to be buried among my own."

"Your ship came in good time for me, Nimrud. Soon

the water will cover all the West, even unto the Arimaneans."

Nimrud again closed his eyes, and spoke as from a long way off: "I am already dead. I hunted men among the Sethians and lost my way, falling from a high place. Then my death ship came for me."

Perscors puzzled it out. "Why did the ship not take you straight to your death?"

"I do not know. Perhaps Saklas holds me between life and death, perhaps it is some other Archon."

Perscors spoke with great bitterness: "Why would Saklas punish a mighty hunter before the Lord, a servant of the Archons, a slayer of men?"

Opening his eyes, Nimrud stared at Perscors for a long time. "You have the look of another hunter of men. I serve Arimanes, not Saklas. Whom do you serve?"

"I do not serve," Perscors asserted. He continued to stare at Nimrud. Then he noticed the speeding up of the bark. The waves flew back in response, but ahead and to every side now there was only ocean. The water was so dark that Perscors could not tell from it if it was night or day.

"Nimrud, can I steer this ship?"

The hunter smiled, but only with his eyes. "Our ship has no rudder, wanderer, and we are driven on by a wind that blows from Siniavis, from the icy regions of death."

CHAPTER 29

Riding the Flood; Norea

O L A M , O N his raft, was carried on swiftly, farther to the west. Innumerable flights of birds passed over him, all going northward. Only the doves seemed to be flying in his direction.

Brooding on the corpses of men, women, and children, and the carcasses of beasts, all flowing past him, Olam felt his anger grow to an extent where he tried to compel himself not to see any longer.

"I came here for the one purpose, to recover my tower, and to purge Valentinus by it. I am not here to save a doomed world."

But this growling inner negation did not convince Olam himself. He stared on, and could not harden his feelings to the horror. Saklas had formed these creatures, they were his, and yet he drowned them, not even for sport: they happened to be in the path of the wanderers who had come to Lucifer.

Olam, borne on in the darkness, contemplated the mystery of the Demiurge. What did Saklas fear? Whom did he fear most? Was this flood for Olam and Valentinus, who had experience in evading catastrophes, or for the untried but invariably capable Perscors?

"For all of us together," Olam muttered into the gray-whiteness of dawn. The flood surged on, yet peering west he saw mountain peaks hovering above the waters. There he would beach his raft, and further contemplate the dilemmas of his blocked quest.

By what should have been mid-afternoon, he rested upon a particularly broad crag, where he secured his raft. Climbing up, he had heard a woman's voice, but he waited for her to find him.

As he did so, he entered upon the deepest of his reveries. It was back before the Beginnings that he had walked in the Pleroma. Even there, in that Fullness, an impatience had lodged in him, though not as strongly as it had in Achamoth. Perhaps, in him, not an impatience but a *forwardness*, a desire to anticipate and to prevent the catastrophe of the Beginnings, of that Creation which was also a Fall. The first flood, he remembered now, had been sent by the Archons as cruelly as this flood had been launched upon the harsh world of Lucifer. Olam's mind lapsed into a reverie of darkness.

A woman's voice, gentle, urgent, and distantly familiar, startled Olam out of what had become a trance.

"If you are what you seem to be, one of the Aeons, wise and benevolent, then help us now against this westward flood!"

Olam blinked as the drowning world of Lucifer came back into focus. In the later moments of his trance, he had forgotten everything: the crag, the flood, the quest, and his separated companions. The woman robed in blue who stood before him was slight and very fair. In her face Olam read no desperation, but only knowledge and dignity.

"I am Olam, one of the Everlasting. But this is not my world. I am pledged to act here only to recover what is my own."

The woman's response sounded forth with an intensity that startled Olam: "Though mortal, I too am from the Alien God! Will you drift by and let Saklas drown out all those who know that he is a usurper? Do you visit a world only to provoke the Archons to fresh torments upon the helpless?"

Olam frowned angrily, but knew that his anger was not against the woman. He had not gone down to earth, and then out to Lucifer, to redeem multitudes, but only to recall Valentinus to an abandoned mission, and even that goal was for earth alone.

Yet this nameless woman, he reflected, spoke only the truth. He had brought Valentinus here, in search of a single tower, a place of purgation and recovery into re-birth. But he had brought a living man, Perscors, as well as the reincarnated form of a dead prophet requiring a sojourn in the place of rest. Perhaps he had meant Pers-cors to terrify the Archons, to distract them from the passage of Valentinus and from his own journey.

The woman watched him patiently and reverently, as he brooded on. How little he understood even of his own strength! He did not even know the source of Perscors's evident powers, though he sensed uneasily that the giant was a version of Primal Man come back, if the Manichean fable was to be believed.

His attention returned to the woman who stood before him. If the Demiurge, in his terror, drowned thousands in this sparsely populated world, was not part of the blame due to Olam himself?

He spoke to the woman, slowly and reluctantly, but with a gruff chagrin to his tone: "You speak the truth. What Saklas has done, I cannot undo, but wherever I can, I will save the victims. And you I will take with me, from this crag to the far West."

She inclined her head in acceptance, but did not speak. Helping her down to his raft, Olam again was troubled by half-perceived memories. He began to understand that he also, and not just Valentinus, suffered from lost remembrances. He had spoken to this woman before, in one of her earlier incarnations, and on earth, not on Lucifer. And then he remembered.

"You are called Norea."

She nodded in confirmation, but kept silence. As they rode the flood together, Olam mused upon that earlier Norea, whose breath had burned the ark of earth's Demiurge three times, until she was allowed to ride through to survival upon it.

Overhead the birds continued to fly northward, except for the doves, joined now by some ravens, who still followed his course. Olam, troubled, began to wonder what waited for him in the West.

CHAPTER **30**

Mystery of Mithra

PERSCORS AWOKE in darkness, to find himself alone upon the hunter Nimrud's death ship. Either the hunter had been washed away while Perscors slept or else some Archon had intervened to claim his own.

How long he had voyaged, or even whether it was night or day, Perscors could not tell. The torrential rains continued to fall, and the death ship went swiftly onward.

Blue-white rays began to sweep the sky. Perscors glanced back at what he took to be the east, and watched the rays develop into a huge flower of light. Hatred energized him as he studied the Demiurge's triumph of self-celebration. For the first time on Lucifer, Perscors decided that his quest now had a clear aim: to battle against the Archons, though it be in no cause and to no purpose.

The strengthening light revealed that Nimrud had left behind not only the purple mantle that had been his shroud but his weapons also. A great bow, a quiver with a dozen arrows, and a huge jagged lance lay at Perscors's feet. The hunter of men had been a seven-foot giant, but Perscors was scarcely half a foot shorter. With the mantle wrapped around him for warmth, and grimly armed for the next violence that this world of religion would hurl against him, he faced west.

Full day had come behind him. Overhead the doves flew westward. Perscors realized that he had slept for some days, and that his voyage was nearing an end.

In a few hours the rains suddenly ceased. Peering ahead, he made out what seemed a coast. The Demiurge's deluge had stopped short of whatever peoples lay there. Perscors felt no anxiety about Valentinus, who perhaps had gotten through the floods before him, and at the thought of Olam, he smiled, wondering how that rough and impatient being had ridden on to his goal. But the smile vanished suddenly, as Perscors remembered his dream about north being the true direction. He shrugged, and leaned heavily upon Nimrud's lance to brace himself as the battered bark ran aground with a crash that splintered its sides.

Perscors marched forward into swampy ground, which gradually rose to a high plain, from which the cold light revealed hills rising ahead. A sense of futility, of the possibility of repetition, came to him from the slant of the light falling upon those hills. A raven flew close by his left ear, and then circled about the base of the nearest rise.

He quickened his march, keeping the raven in sight. Suddenly it seemed to dart into the hill, disappearing within a cave entrance. Perscors came up to the opening; statues flanked the dark mouth he hesitated to enter. To one side was a five-foot dark marble statue of a naked, lion-headed being, six times entwined by a serpent, whose head rested upon the being's skull. Four wings with emblems of the seasons upon them extended from the statue's back; each of its hands held a key. Upon its breast, a thunderbolt was engraved, and along the base Perscors made out a hammer and tongs, and the wand of Hermes, two snakes curled around a scepter. The statue gazed at Perscors as though it were mocking him. He grinned back at it with disdain, and turned his glance to the other statue.

This was a bas-relief in white marble, nearly as wide as its five-foot height. At its center a young god sacrificed a bull, plunging a broad dagger into its throat, while grasping a horn. The face of the god, though expressionless, troubled Perscors, who felt reminded of a past danger. To each side of the sacrifice, a youth stood against what seemed the decorated wall of a cave. The youth at the left bore an uplifted torch; one held by his counterpart pointed downward. On the cave's wall, Perscors could identify images of a snake, a dog, and a raven.

But he could read them only in the crudest sense, and shrugging off what he could not comprehend, Perscors entered the high cave, lance at the ready. No sooner in than he was dazzled by light, as though of a brighter sun than Lucifer could ever offer. Before him was a massive rock of white marble, with a knife embedded at its summit. Shifting Nimrud's lance to his left hand, Perscors drew the knife from the rock without difficulty. Though very sharp, it had a ceremonial look, being made of some shining material he could not identify. Upon its hilt he read the single word NABARZE, unknown to any of his memories.

"The knife is here to some purpose," he said, and then he added, "So am I." As he looked around the surprisingly large dimensions of the brightly lit cave, he became disturbed at his inability to trace the source of the illumination. The prescience of battle came to him, and with it the awareness that his enemy or enemies were not human. He placed his lance carefully against the cave wall, and removed quiver and bow also. Wrapping the mantle more closely about him, and tightening his grip on the knife, he went forward slowly, into greater depths.

"Is it a world or a cave?" he muttered, after what seemed an hour's advance into nothingness. The grotto was unchanged and endless, except that as he went on, the glare became more intense.

"A cold light," he murmured, and then the thought came to him that he was walking in the realm of an interior sun, in a day that had not been the work of Saklas. This is my sun, and though cold it is unconquered. Better to be here, in the light of my own sun, than to be warm in the common light of every day on earth.

But the invisibility of his sun troubled him. He was here in this grotto to perform his own act, and not the will of god or demons, but something in what loomed ahead might occur much against his will. Directly as he sensed his danger, the raven—and whose messenger was it?—appeared again and brushed his side.

"My own sun sends me the raven so that I may kill what must be killed."

He thought of the bas-relief and shuddered despite himself. An old horror came back to him from his earthly life: it was a sickness that he had felt about bullfighting. But he had not long to suffer such memories, such anticipation.

A bull, huge and black, manifesting itself as if from nowhere, rushed forcefully at him. Perscors seized the beast by its nostrils with one hand, while with the other he plunged deep into its flank the ritual hunting knife.

But the force of the beast's onrush was greater than he had expected. He avoided the horns, but lost the knife, and was thrown violently against the cave wall. When he scrambled up, the black bull was well beyond him and rushing toward the cave's mouth. Perscors followed, but stopped to retrieve the bow, quiver, and lance of Nimrud. When he stepped out of the cave's mouth, the beast was not in sight, but a small half circle of armed men in white tunics confronted him. Arrows sped by Perscors as he withdrew inside the cave.

CHAPTER **31**

Mithraeans and Arimaneans

A FAMILIAR rage strengthened Perscors. The skill of archery, unpracticed for many years, returned to him as if through Nimrud's bow itself. Without taking conscious aim, he drew the head of an arrow to his fist, handling it with ease. The arrow hit one of the white-clad warriors under the chin, and punched up through his throat. Within a few moments, the others had fled out of range.

"Like Nimrud, I am best at hunting men. But who these are, and why they attack me, are only fresh signs of my ignorance."

He came forth from the cave, and went up to the corpse. The quiver of the slain man bore the word NABARZE. Had these warriors attacked him because they judged him an impostor? Or because they thought him to be Nimrud, or another Arimanean? Arimanes he remembered now as another name for the evil principle. From old knowledge, there came back to him the name of the bull-slaying god whom he had failed to emulate: Mithras. The dead man must be a Mithraean.

"I fight on the wrong side," Perscors muttered. He was suddenly very weary. Finding Valentinus could be the only goal for him, to dissolve somehow, through their meeting, the frustrations of this disordered quest.

Resolutely he set himself westward again over the hills, which were becoming higher. Some hours farther on, he put an arrow through a kind of wild pig and made a melancholy feast. He neglected to put out the fire at which he had roasted the pig, but fell asleep, wrapped in Nimrud's mantle and resting upon the giant hunter's lance.

Some hours later, when he woke abruptly, only its embers showed forth in the gradually waning darkness. A dream in which Olam's yellow face, fierce with anger, was shouting at him, fled with Perscors's awareness of approaching men. Stamping out the embers, he hid in a thicket in the hollow between two hills.

A cluster of purple-clad warriors arrived and gathered around the remnants of his fire and his feast. In the morning's uncertain light, he counted eight—tall men but, except for one, closer to his own height than to the giant Nimrud's. They too were armed with lance and bow, except for the tallest, who carried an outsize battle-ax.

Eight, Perscors decided, were too many devil worshippers to attack at once. Better, he thought, to stalk them first, then pick enough of them off to make a direct attack possible later. That they marched westward anyway, after leaving the site, made his decision simpler.

He waited until they were beyond his gaze, and then walked west. The hills began to be wooded, more and more thickly, and gradually Perscors came to realize that the light had been changing. A purplish haze had hovered wherever he looked, but by now it seemed to have become one with the atmosphere.

"Here, beyond the flood, this planet no longer is ruled by Saklas. Is this, then, the world of Arimanes?"

He had spoken aloud, and was startled by what seemed an answering wind around his ears. A dark memory came to him, and he stared up at the treetops, half expecting to see Nekbael floating above him. The wind swept strongly through the woods.

As Perscors moved forward, slowly and uncertainly, he stumbled against a dark object, about the size of the head of a yearling calf. Bending down, he raised it by a stiff, tasseled handle. It was a rude drum, made of some tanned hide stretched over a metal frame. The whole frame, roughly shaped like an inverted, truncated pyramid, peculiarly resembled both a bovine head and the shadow of a kind of harp.

The desire to beat upon it rose strongly in Perscors; given the incessant sound of the wind, he could not believe that the Arimaneans, up ahead of him, would be able to hear. He turned the drum on its side and found again the word of Mithras: NABARZE. Holding the drum, he became aware that the word meant something like "unconquered" or "victorious." Was the hide that of a black bull like the one he had failed to kill?

"This too," he murmured, "is here to some purpose, to serve me. But how?"

He kept the drum in his left hand and went forward through the mists, feeling his way with Nimrud's lance. The hills grew higher, and at last the purple of the haze wearied his eyes to the point of blindness. Suddenly he felt no ground ahead as he probed. The mists cleared enough to give him a startled glimpse of a ravine, upon whose edge he precariously verged. As the mists cleared further, he saw a rope bridge suspended over the ravine.

When Perscors came to the bridge, he found it swaying uncertainly across the abyss. Had the Arimaneans crossed just before him, or was this a trap?

The mists cleared away, to and then beyond the other side of the chasm, revealing a tall man, as tall as Nimrud, standing at the bridge's farther end. Robed in purple, he carried an immense battle-ax. As Perscors watched, this warrior started toward him.

Stunned, Perscors saw that the giant was walking not on, but somehow at least a foot above the ramp of the bridge. Though his first impulse was to charge across toward this being, a deeper drive spoke in Perscors: this was not a man but a demon or a god, to be fought, but not with spear or with arrows. As he watched the floating advance of his adversary, Perscors calmly put down Nimrud's lance, laid aside the bow and quiver, and marched onto the swaying bridge holding the Mithraean drum in his left hand, and beating it with his right fist.

At the first drumbeat, the giant with the battle-ax sank to ground himself on the bridge but continued his advance. As Perscors steadily approached, still beating the drum, the purple-robed warrior hesitated.

With only some seven feet between them, Perscors paused, fascinated and troubled by the fierce, bearded face. Its eyes were enormous, the complexion purplish, almost black.

"Into the abyss with you, wanderer!"

The shrill, screeching cry seemed to come at Perscors from all directions at once.

An awful calm rose in Perscors. He steadily struck the drum and moved closer to the demon. An exultant flame moved in his spirit, and he knew a joy greater than any he had known before on Lucifer.

The demonic face before him suddenly enlarged, while the mists closed in again. As the battle-ax came sharply down at him, Perscors leaned to the right and thrust the narrower bottom of the drum with terrible backhand force into the raging, purplish face. The ax went by Perscors and fell into the abyss. So did the drum; they fell to the far bottom without sound. Perscors found himself alone on the middle of the wildly swaying bridge, with no sense or belief of having thrown his opponent off the bridge. Rather, he began to suspect that the demon had chosen to vanish, perhaps to ambush Perscors on the other side.

Ought he not go back, to retrieve Nimrud's weapons? Perscors shrugged, and made his way across the bridge, to the other side. Seven Arimaneans would be less of a menace than their demon-leader, who now seemed only a trickster and a coward.

Only when he stood on the other side did the thought come to Perscors that he did not know who his opponent had been. What did it matter, he mused in contempt, since the force within him could overcome whatever rose against him? Even if the sun of Mithras proved not to be his sun, an inward fire would guard and guide him until he died.

"Until I die?" he questioned. So then, he *was* to die, here on Lucifer? But not before battering at and at least maiming the Archons, and not before serving some purpose of which he sensed Valentinus to be the manifestation. Impatient to master the full range of his fate, he marched westward through the hills. Before him Mithraeans and Arimaneans alike shuddered as they lay in useless ambush. They would go back to their wars again when this mumbling terror of a wanderer had passed them by. The icy wind of death blew on with Perscors, who had crossed the bridge of Sinvat against Arimanes himself, and whose fate it was to carry blindly to an end the revenge of earth against the stars.

CHAPTER **32**

Revels of Nekbael

A T D A W N , Perscors emerged into a green valley, cut
through by a lake that seemed to be a violently eddying
river. Even in the clear light, he could not make out the
precise contours of it; it was extensive enough to vanish
into the horizon. But the vista was less strange than the
sight of a giant black stone mill at the lake's edge. As he
came up to this huge structure, Perscors distinctly heard
a noise of grinding, though there were no signs of people
about.

"A demonic mill? Grinding away to produce what?
And why here?"

The questions were partly answered after a few
glances as he stood at the lake's edge. The workings of

the mill were evidently partly underground, since the grinding action was generating a whirlpool in the lake. Perscors brought some of the water to his lips. It appeared that the mill ground out salt, as well as the maelstrom which, eddying out into the lake, seemed darker than it should be, and almost reddish.

Somewhere, on earth, Perscors remembered seeing such a mill, though hardly on this absurd scale. The memory came back to him of a water mill he had come upon once in the Orkney Islands. But there a stream had agitated the mill; here the churning seemed to create an ocean out of a lake. Time, which on Lucifer had become indefinite for him, weighed upon Perscors again because of the oppressiveness of this mill. Not once, he reflected, had he studied the night sky of Lucifer: time and the stars had fled together. Was it that he had learned Olam's contempt for the world of clocks and starlight? Troubled, he resolved to watch the sky carefully that night, if it were clear, as it promised to be.

He looked up at the mill. It seemed even more grotesquely gigantic: ought he to enter it? He felt profound dread; realizing this provoked his fury. What on Lucifer had the power to frighten him? Perhaps a knowledge that he wished to avoid?

"Here," he mused, "is a mill that grinds by itself and turns by itself. It is much too large to be of human origin or use. Who made it, then?"

As he stared up at it again, he had the illusion that it towered up more each time he focused upon it. He could hardly see now where it ended and where the sky began. "The maker was Saklas," he muttered, and with that declaration he resolved to enter and explore the mill, which, in its changing perspective, now looked more like a huge tower with a waterwheel attached than a proper mill.

A walk around it revealed no obvious entrance, which was unsurprising to Perscors, who supposed there to be a covert, underground way in. But circuit after circuit disclosed nothing; short of digging away at the foundations of the entire mill—an endless task—he was baffled. He stood by the lake again and studied the whirlpool. If the pillar was not to be climbed, was the way in through the water? How did one descend without being churned away?

"I am not fool enough to enter your maelstrom, Saklas." But his hoarse voice was overheard. An answering voice, mocking and female, spoke from just by Perscors's right ear. "Who gives the measures, you or Saklas?"

Perscors spun around enraged, but he was alone, or seemed to be. This world, he thought, turns under Saklas; he is its millstone. But this world held no sway over Olam, or over Valentinus, and it had little enough power over Perscors, despite all its apparent efforts.

"Saklas moves every handle here," Perscors deliberately said aloud, hoping to raise the female voice again; he met silence. From somewhere he remembered an ancient remark to the effect that heaven turns around like a millstone, and always does something bad.

The answer to Saklas's sway came to Perscors suddenly, and sang his spirit to the combat: "Fire, my fire, will burn through this pillar of the sky. Fire will end the grinding of this mill."

His ecstatic shout raised a wind against him. Dashed against the mill's stone wall, he rose up vowing silently that the mill itself, if he could partly burn it, would sink into its own whirlpool. But how to burn a vast closed building of massive black stone? Only interminably and from within, until it toppled over into the waters. He was back to the puzzle of finding the way inside it. One of the stone blocks must be movable, if only by enchantment which he could not direct, but perhaps by force as well. He set out to discover the potential opening.

The wind continued with great intensity, and Perscors struggled to keep upright against the eddying motion whirling about him, which it now assumed. He stumbled on a stone, and fell across it; scrambling up, he remembered the Sunday-school text: "Whosoever shall fall upon that stone shall be broken," and was grimly thankful that this was not literal prophecy. But then he remembered the text prior to it: "The stone which the builders refused is become the headstone of the corner." Perscors assumed that he must discover the imperfect cornerstone.

Still ruminating, Perscors went up to the mill's northwest corner. He pushed hard against the cornerstone, and slid it easily to one side. The way in was here, and its darkness did not disconcert him. Though unarmed, and bending over, he entered readily and cheerfully, intent upon the mill's destruction.

There was a glimmering light ahead, fitful and unfocused. It was enough for Perscors to make his way by, but it sputtered out after he had walked only a few steps. He paused, sensing again that he had to descend, and awaiting an intuition of the way. The voice of the mocking woman sounded again to his right: "I asked you once if I was to tell you old stories? Do you remember?"

"How could I forget?" Perscors replied. "It is all you ever have said to me."

"I left my ring in your gauntlet," she whispered, her lips now touching his right ear.

"Probably the Marcionites stole it." His voice was harsh, but the desire for her otherness overcame him again. He moved suddenly to his left, away from her, and spoke with deliberate roughness. "You nearly killed me twice. No one but you in this world of damnation has come so close to ending me."

Her voice came to him as the most graceful of mockeries, almost as song: "You are to die here on Lucifer, anyway. Take death's pleasure with me."

His laughter was so violent that the pain of it surprised him; he stepped still farther away. "Decidedly you are very dangerous. I have learned not to grapple with you. But take a friendly enough warning. I get stronger each day on Lucifer. You might not win this time."

Her answering laughter faded away, until he knew that she had left him. But her manifestation confirmed his conviction of the mill's malice. He listened deeply to his own silence, hoping to hear the voice of his knowing self, rather than his questing self. A slow, almost hissing syllable came; "fire" was the word. And so he need only seek a fire. Moving off to his left he saw a flickering light again, and walked slowly toward it. When he came up to it, he stopped in bafflement.

What sprawled before him was a ruined forge, the charcoal smoldering, as though the hearth had been recently in use. What smith had worked within this mill, and to what purpose?

Here was fire for the taking.

"But it is not my fire," Perscors murmured. Nor was it the fire he longed to steal, if such burned on Lucifer. He was filled with deep disdain. "Fire stolen from Saklas is good for one thing only—to consume what serves Saklas." After speaking, Perscors seized a knobby wooden club from the hearth and held it upon the charcoal, until it flared up violently.

Holding this torch before him, Perscors walked away from the forge, moving toward the sound of the grinding. When it was most intense, he paused, looked about, and found a loose stone block in the floor. He raised it, moved it aside, and saw a narrow stair winding downward.

Torch in his left hand, and right fist ready, Perscors descended. And then horror assailed him from every side: Nekbael was nowhere to be seen, but the victims of her revels were piled up like cordwood, end to end; gashed and battered heads and necks lay alongside twisted feet. Dazed and sickened, Perscors did not pause to count the corpses, or the slashes upon each warrior who had died such a cruelly literal love-death.

The great waterwheel churned away beneath him, turned in the lake water by a process Perscors did not wish to learn. Above was stone, but the underground structure holding the wheel was wood and fit to burn. Wherever the torch could be applied, he did so, until many fires smoldered, finally caught, and flamed until, hissing loudly in the way of wet wood, the great wheel itself began to smoke and came to rest.

Perscors mounted, and went out through the cornerstone. He did not stay for the slow satisfaction of watching the mill topple at long last into its own whirlpool.

CHAPTER **33**

Escape into the Kenoma

T H E M O O N set early that night, and for the first time
upon Lucifer, Perscors searched the stars. Sitting upon
the highest hill that he could find, overlooking a steep
valley, he sensed that his westward way must soon end
and that his solitude would not prevail much longer. The
moon of Lucifer, he had realized earlier, was as much
brighter than the moon of earth as the sun of Lucifer
was more pallid than the earthly one. Now, unfamiliar as
he found the patterns of glitter in the starry night to be,
Perscors was startled to behold, in the northwest quarter
of the sky, a pale swath of what seemed a version of the
Milky Way.

He remembered reading somewhere of a Northern
tribe that called the Milky Way "the tracks of God." Was

this frail zone of light like that other, a path for the Demiurge? Was the heart of the Milky Way yet one more whirlpool of destruction?

No sense of an earthly Sublime remained in him as he glared at these heavens. He felt their total hostility, and began to imagine that they were scowling back at him, and through their darknesses, rather than with the gentle fancy of starry eyes. Who was he to challenge these vast spaces and intervening brilliances? Sleep overcame him. In his dream he was wandering through Saklas's mill, searching for a ferryman.

"But to find the ferryman, I must name him!"

His own despairing cry woke him for a second. Perscors blinked up at the mocking light of the stars. A moment passed, and he slept again.

Was the ferryman Olam? No fire stirred in that naming. Perscors wandered on through labyrinthine turnings of corridors in the mill's interior. But the imprint of no other name touched him.

He floated now in the churning of the Milky Way. "It is grinding *away* from me," he muttered, and wondered what he himself meant by "It." The name? A mountain loomed ahead of him. Towering high, higher than the mill, the mountain was an immense churning club. When the churning mountain flared up, Perscors merged with it, and then was awake.

He rose unsteadily, resolving not to sleep again. The dream had done what he had thought could not be done: he had been made afraid. Not of Saklas, or of Arimanes, or of any other Archon: it could only be of himself. Perscors looked down into the valley. The glance revealed a whole cluster of purple-clad, marching forms moving toward the south base of his hill. Glints of metal flashed faintly and almost impossibly at him in the starry night.

"Arimaneans, perhaps twenty or thirty of them. And I am unarmed."

For a few moments, he contemplated holding his position and defending it by a hail of stones. But a battle with mere men, even with crazed idolaters of a crazier devil, seemed unworthy of him. His true strife was to be with powers, and he disdained any slaughter of mere Arimanean believers, however brutal their pieties. "Let them call it an escape," he growled, and began a rapid descent of the hill to its north base.

It was hours later, as he judged, when he realized that he had begun to move through a wholly different terrain. The muddy wastes of the Kenoma stretched all about him. A great exhilaration came over him in his north-ward march: knowledge that the true way led in this direction could not fail to come as well to Olam and to Valentinus.

At dawn he realized that the Arimaneans had pursued him into the Kenoma. Shouts behind him met answering cries from in front and off to his right. Perscors veered left until he came to a patch of rocky ground in the midst of the soft Kenoma. In the sure knowledge of his fortune, he calmly looked around for a weapon. Against the highest rock someone had heaped up a pile, half as tall as he, of rounded stones. Perscors weighed one in each hand. They would do for missiles, if the Arimaneans came close enough, but how was he to dodge their arrows? Best to go forward nonetheless, he decided, and arm himself from his pursuers.

With a rock in each hand, he turned toward them, in the murk of early light. Glancing up, he found himself grateful for the cloudiness of the morning, and for the mists gathering over the Kenoma. Raising one of the stones, Perscors smashed it square into the face of an Arimanean who had appeared just before him. The man went down, and Perscors fell with him, as the javelin of another warrior went by him overhead. He moved sharply to crush the back of that one's head with a sweep of his other stone, and then swung instantly to lance through another oncoming Arimanean with the javelin he had recovered from the ground. Gathering his victims' quivers, a bow, and a lance, he turned back to confront whoever dared to move against him.

But there were no more shouts, and no one came to the combat. The lust to kill now burned in Perscors, and lacking more victims, he shouted in rage. But these roars of fury drove off the other Arimaneans, who fled what seemed to them a hopeless struggle against an unknown demon. Frustrated in and by his wrath, Perscors turned to resume his northern march. As the anger slowly waned, there grew in its place the cold feeling that a subtler trial awaited him somewhere up ahead, concealed within the emptiness.

CHAPTER **34**

Loss of Ruha

W H E N T H E sun was directly overhead, Perscors
halted. The tract of the Kenoma across which he had
traveled had led on to high ground in the north—bleaker
heights than any he had seen upon Lucifer. Bare black
cliffs rose in most places to form a barrier so sheer as to
seem insurmountable. He came up to the base, and after
an hour there discerned a way up, long and narrow and
zigzagging between switchbacks. Sometime later, climbing with great difficulty along the rock-littered path, he
heard his name being called. Unable to locate the
woman's voice, or even decide the direction it came
from, he kept on.

In the softer light of evening, he reached a more inviting upland, a place of rolling meadows among which wandered a single placid stream. He drank of its cold, dark water, finding it bitter, then lay down to rest, weakened by hunger and by his relentless march. He knew now that to keep on in this way was to become either a beast or a god.

"Perhaps I am a mixture of both." The gloomy hoarseness of his own voice startled him. Ruha's voice, soft and urgent, sounded in reply: "You cannot become an Archon if you insist upon opposing the Archons."

Rising and spinning about, he could not see her, and again could not locate the place of the voice. No one was in sight. Did her voice accompany him as a spell, or was she hidden somehow behind or within this deceptive landscape? Or was he haunted by her hmurthas, invisible handmaidens who moved upon the winds? They would have the trick of her voice.

"But do I want her still? I fled her, on her terms."

His bare whisper provoked her reply, coming now with greater urgency.

"How can you know of want? For what are you but a ceaseless want, a fire that cannot procreate?"

Bewilderment diffused through his spirit, which could now know neither grief nor fear; then consternation came strongly upon him.

Perscors turned around, shouting bitterly to every side: "Have the courage to show yourself! If you want to speak to me, then come and speak directly!"

But there was no reply. Perscors gathered himself together, cast off the shock, and marched north out of the meadow. The night was clear again, but he did not deign to look up: the rational fire of the stars did not interest him. His own fire might be dark with ignorance, but he knew it to give a better light than the cosmos could afford him.

Just before dawn, he slept for a little while, having come to a place where the land, beneath increasingly heavy underbrush, began quite suddenly to slope sharply downward. Voices of men woke him, and he concealed himself in a thicket to observe who these might be. In the thin light, a party of hunters filed past him, going north. Whoever these were, they were not Arimaneans or any other people that Perscors had seen on Lucifer. Their cloaks, apparently of sheepskin, were gray, and along with the bows slung behind them, they carried long horsemen's lances. Some fifty of them stalked by him and vanished in the undergrowth ahead. These wild men, long-haired and desperate-looking, seemed too numerous to have formed only a hunting expedition. A war patrol, perhaps?

"Scythians," came Ruha's voice in his ear. "Scythian horsemen, going back to their mounts, and then to the lands in the North." She stood next to him, as first he had seen her, half mocking, half beckoning. A great weariness came over him, augmenting his hunger and his bewilderment.

"Speak, if you have something I should hear."

But she stood silently, lips slightly parted, as though awaiting either his anger or his surrender. Even in his exhaustion, Perscors held back from either reaction; a resolve to follow the Scythians to the North took their place. There fulfillment would come to him, and not with this half-treacherous child of Achamoth. Yet, as always, he yearned for her; something incomplete in him had been touched by her. When she spoke, at last, he was startled by the flow of her language and its tone, which seemed to recite an old story but with the immediacy of an intimate instruction given only to him.

"My mother, Achamoth, begot a thought on herself. Her desire was to make a likeness, but without the consent of the Spirit who was her husband, for he did not approve. Her power was invincible, and her desire did not remain idle. But the thing that came out of her was not perfect, and was like her and unlike her as well. When Achamoth saw the work of her desire, it had changed into the semblance of a serpent with the face of a lion, and its eyes flashed with the fire of the stars.

"Achamoth cast it away from her, so that it lay outside her place, where no one of the Aeons could see it; for she had made it in her ignorance. And she enclosed it in a luminous cloud, and in the midst of the cloud she placed a throne, that only she might see it. And she called his name Saklas. This was the first Archon; he took great power from his mother. And he removed himself from her and away from her places.

"Out of himself he made the world. And took his sister, the daughter of Achamoth, as his wife . . ."

This recitation infuriated Perscors. "I know all this and more. But what are you trying to tell me? What have I to do with you?"

She looked at him more directly than before. Bewilderment worked in her features; she struggled to speak, but it was as if her face would not let her.

Perscors pointed north. "I go there to put an end to my misadventures. What belongs to the Aeons, and to me, must be taken back from Saklas. If you would leave Saklas and come with me, then come. But only if indeed you can and will leave him."

She stared at him, and then was able to answer very

softly, but only with a question that, it seemed to Perscors, it was too late to ask: "But what are *you*? Are you here only to burn yourself away? Are you one of the Everlasting?"

Perscors wondered at how little he felt just at this moment. The pain of this parting was being postponed; there might be time, before the end, to know that pain truly. He searched for the words of truth and grace, but a hoarse whisper emerged from him instead. He was speaking only to himself.

"What I am will be shown, by and to me, before this place and I are quit of each other. Much will be burned away with me, if I vanish into my own fire. Fear will come upon the Archons in my presence, fear of the pre-existent man who is in me, and who was not created by the Demiurge. They will be terrified, and in their terror the Archons will rush to conceal, and then to ruin, their work."

She stepped back and away from him, her eyes like locked, unshining doors. Perscors turned from her, knowing it was for the last time, and resumed his search for his own place.

CHAPTER 35

End of the Way West

AFTER HE had sailed to where the slowly receding flood waters ended, Olam did not march inland. He bade farewell to Norea and his other orphans plucked from the waves, and wandered south along the margin of the flood—a wide shore, in what had once been a broad valley, but was now ringed closely with low cliffs. Uneasiness, which he had known so rarely, now wandered with him. He had come down to earth to recover Valentinus, and out to Lucifer to reclaim his own place of rest, his own share in the Pleroma. But the way had been more difficult than he had prophesied, and his own memory now seemed as maimed as the memory of Valentinus.

As he walked away from the water, he mused aloud:

"I have been duped since I landed here. What I seek is not in the West, no matter how far I go."

He was closer to the cliffs than he had realized, and his growing self-chastisement echoed back to him: "How far I go," but the words were now an affirming sigh. He looked up and studied the rocks above him. Before the flood had lapped so far, there had been a cleft through them. It was time, he decided, to rejoin Valentinus.

Olam turned around and stared north along the shore. He had not walked long when a glance out toward the ebbing flood showed him a small boat approaching. Without curiosity or elation, he stood quietly as Valentinus ran the craft aground. They stared at one another. Valentinus came ashore in the robes of a priest of Ennoia, having appropriated them from the stone chamber of the disguised Saklas. Olam was in Manichean garb, having borrowed it from one of the refugees picked up by his raft. Intent and puzzled as ever, Valentinus disregarded the grim laughter of the Aeon at the misleading garments that covered each of them, like inadvertent falsehoods.

"Old friend, two survivors like ourselves can laugh a little at the oddness of what we take on."

Valentinus ignored the remark, and stated his own concerns: "Olam, where is Perscors now? And where do we go next?"

Exasperated, Olam kicked at a feeble tongue of wave: "By Achamoth's vile womb, I don't know the answer to either! Your friend is probably this side of the flood by now, whoring away and killing, as usual! Doubtless, he is with Nekbael, or Ruha, or even Achamoth herself. Or with some other Lilith. Or he is frightening Arimanes, or whatever Archon is in these parts, and he is slaughtering their idolaters by the bushel. What does it matter—he will get worse until he is crazed altogether, and dead of his madness."

Valentinus's voice was cold in reply: "Did you bring him here for that?"

Olam grew more irate. "He has what he wants! How can I know what the wretch will turn into before he is done? I seem to have lost some memories myself! What he was back there in the origins, I don't know. But probably not human, anyway . . ."

Olam grinned uncertainly as his voice trailed off. Valentinus continued to scowl, but the impasse broke as Olam's mood changed. He shrugged, and spoke more soberly: "Old friend, we shall go to the North. He who was Thomas Perscors may get there before us. The trick of this world is that it repeats earth, but very belatedly! When there was a remnant of the Pleroma on earth, it always lay beyond the north wind."

Valentinus experienced another return of memory. "They used to say that the land of the Hyperboreans, beyond the north wind, was beyond the wandering Scythians, who neither plow nor sow."

Olam laughed mirthlessly. "Be assured that Saklas is no more inventive than earth's Demiurge, Ialdabaoth. Between us and the windless land, as on earth, the worst of his minions will be found; no matter—Perscors will burn through them ahead of us, and we will push through against the remnant."

He turned his eyes up to the cliffs, saying: "I cannot trust this new shoreline. We must climb north. You are as good a scrambler in rocky places as I am."

Valentinus, as they moved to higher ground, remembered better the old stories of Scythians and Hyperboreans: "We are going against the shamans, against Abaris and Aristaeus."

"Excellent," rejoined Olam. "They are fair game for you, and even an amusement for me, if indeed they survive Perscors long enough to entertain us."

He led the way, springing among the rocks with remarkable agility. But Valentinus, following with effort, was absorbed in an inner bafflement again. Whatever this quest was, it seemed not to need him. The image of a man riding upon an arrow wavered before him. He shook his head impatiently, and concentrated upon keeping up with his vehement guide.

CHAPTER **36**

Voyage to the Hyperboreans

PERSCORS HAD followed the Scythians for only an hour when they came out of the undergrowth onto the bank of a narrow river, which must have been quite deep, as the waters moved very slowly. A small group of their company awaited them with a wide raft, which some of them boarded; the others clung to its sides as it crossed the deep stream. On the other bank, under the heavy branches of trees, another group of Scythians waited with the full war party's horses and with a boat-wagon. Concealed among rushes, watching the crossing, Perscors wondered how he was to go on following them.

When they had landed and quickly cleared the other bank, moving beyond his sight among the trees, Perscors went down to the river. He drank some of the water, which was pleasant to the taste. Low-growing branches, like those of stunted fig trees, bore a peculiar fruit, bean-shaped berries, varying in hue from black to ashy gray. Yet they were sweet and juicy, and Perscors ate as many of them as he could.

A north wind rose forcefully, and troubled the water. He wandered along the river, waiting for a sign. When a crow flew past his right ear, and alighted upon a fruit tree, the sign was evident. Perscors approached the tree and the crow simply vanished before his eyes. Turning then from the tree toward the river, he saw a grotesque old man squatting before him on the ground: he had not been there before. Naked and tattooed, the old creature grinned toothlessly at Perscors, who felt unease and some disgust. Fawns and snakes alternated in the green and brown tattoo pattern, reaching up the sides of the old man's neck and branching around across his forehead. "Are you here to get me across this river, old one?" He had intended his tone to be jocular, but Perscors felt chagrin as the seriousness of what he had said seemed to echo silently from the damp air itself. The chagrin vanished as the old man's lunatic grin continued; studying him, Perscors knew that he had surmised correctly the tattooed creature's function, and he waited patiently until at last the old man spoke in a high whisper: "I ride across on my arrow."

Still grinning, he produced an arrow from beneath him, whose shaft head and feather seemed to be painted gold, and rammed it at the back of Perscors's left hand. Perscors dodged, and the wound was shallow; but it burned, and he cried aloud. Even as he did so, as if at a signal, the old man disappeared, as swiftly as the crow had vanished.

Perscors picked up the arrow; its weight told him it was all of gold. It was the matter of a few moments for him to use his Arimanean bow to send the shaft speeding across the river. But it fell a few feet short of the other bank. He swam to it, tried to dive for it, failed, and hauled himself up, but without bow or javelin—they had been left on the other side, and he would not return to them now. Leaving his useless quiver behind, he marched through the trees toward the North again, uncomfortably drenched, and with his hand aching. He had no hope of catching up to the Scythian horsemen, and none of stealing a mount from them.

"I need my drum as a horse," he surprised himself by saying. A consciousness of change that was not merely a response to the chill of dampness troubled him, but he compelled himself not to brood upon it. Beyond the hills by the river were open meadows; as he walked across them, he felt a growing weariness, and dropped limply onto the grass. Sleeping where he fell, he dreamed that he was being carried by the north wind to a high place. Before him were seven tents, each with a torn roof, which flapped violently but soundlessly in the wind; he vowed not to enter any of them. The wind caught him up again and carried him higher, until he touched down upon an island surrounded by an endless sea.

The island was treeless and wasted. Perscors stared at seven large, tall stones, placed far apart, and suggesting neither a colonnade nor a ring. He realized that these were the island's holding stones; they would speak to him if he waited, but he resolved not to and called upon the north wind to carry him away again. This time the wind took him to the summit of a high, hemispherical mountain. Perscors descended into a cave which, after a

few feet, gleamed brightly from the mirrors on its walls
and a fire of green flame in the center of a wide chamber,
whose ceiling sloped gradually down to the sides. Before
the fire stood Ruha and Achamoth, each naked. He
understood that they would show him another opening
out of the cave, but unhesitatingly he turned back upward and out the way he had entered. The north wind
came again, and carried him over a desert to a still
higher mountain. This had no easily discernible contour
—cones and humps, high pinnacles vanishing into clouds
presented different aspects as he approached it. He was
set down among some rocks which glinted with a kind of
red mica. There was a cave entrance here, too. When he
entered it, Perscors soon came upon a vast room and a
naked Saklas, working an ugly bellows. On a huge fire
was a brown, rusted caldron, eight feet in diameter.
Saklas saw him, and tried to catch him with a huge pair
of tongs, but Perscors stepped behind a monstrous anvil,
upon which the tongs shattered. Saklas cried out: "Nothing is got for nothing!" But Perscors went out of the cave
and descended with the wind again.

The wind set him down once again upon a river that
flowed north, in a boat shaped like a flat drum, the hide
laced over its frame dyed gray. Whether the skin was
reindeer or horsehide he could not tell, but he saw that
he too now wore gray, like the Scythians. Before him a
gray sail billowed out before the wind, which added its
force to that of the current. A great joy came to Perscors,
but the joy itself throbbed with the beating of a drum
and urged him to wakefulness.

He awoke and looked about him for the thick grass of
the meadow where he had fallen. But he was in a boat,
coursing swiftly through rushing water. It was the gray,

drum-shaped boat of his dream, but he did not doubt its reality now.

"The old shaman put me into a trance with his arrow, and I stole this boat in that trance." He spoke this in defiance to the north wind, but wondered whether he believed himself. He understood that he had somehow refused the initiations of the shaman, and yet had nevertheless won what he needed from that tattooed old grotesque.

A voice almost Achamoth's seemed to speak in the wind, but not distinctly enough for Perscors to make it out. He went back to take the boat's rudder, and now the voice spoke directly into his left ear: "If Abaris sends you to the Hyperboreans, it is for his purposes and not for yours or Olam's."

Perscors shrugged and did not deign to answer. An exultation burned in him; it was as if the very feeling promised him that his purposes were his own. The north wind would take him beyond the north wind, to a place he would proclaim to be his own place, and not the realm of god or of demon.

CHAPTER **37**

The Shamans

PERSCORS STUDIED the more curious features of his boat. A lance decorated with a ladder-like tree pattern rose from its precise middle, below the mast. Perscors attempted to dislodge the lance, for a potential weapon, but he gave up when he discovered that it was strongly wrought into the frame, as if it were another mast. He realized that the cost of the lance must be the breaking apart of the boat. A gray wooden raven was the figurehead, but it broke apart and fell into the water when he tried to examine it closely.

But the most disturbing feature, Perscors felt, was the gray sail. As the wind rose or fell slightly, it changed its shape radically, wrapping itself into cloudlike configurations that, even from as close as he was, could be read for their momentary resemblances: serpent, hog, horse, lion, and owl were among the outlines he could recognize.

Along the river Scythian horsemen shook their spears at him and loosed flights of arrows, but Perscors laughed as his boat sped by them. He had the sense that he voyaged through the sky, though his drum-boat kept to the river. As he got farther north, he began to experience intense cold. The river moved among lofty and precipitous mountains capped with snow. No more Scythians were to be seen, and these northern wastes seemed uninhabitable.

Night came on, and Perscors slept through it though cold and hungry. When he awoke at dawn, he was in another landscape. The river had emptied into the wide bay of some great lake or inland sea. The mountains were blue in the distance—they seemed as fragile as clouds. Nearby gentle hills, covered with groves and orchards, sloped down to the water, all about the shore. The wind had ceased, and his boat had drifted serenely into harbor.

Perscors went ashore to find himself in an olive grove at the foot of one of the soft hills. He devoured a number of olives, and drank water from a nearby spring. The day was windless and bright; groves opened into gardens, all obviously cultivated. But no one was to be seen; he walked on and up through the hills, wondering at the absence of inhabitants. Here was the land beyond the north wind, but where were the Hyperboreans?

As he descended one of the higher rises, Perscors came upon a rough-hewn wooden altar, half concealed by shrubbery. The altar was in the form of a tree-ladder, resembling that decorating the lance at the middle of his drum-boat.

"A shaman is not far off," he muttered, glad of the prospect of some information. A drum beat off to his right, and he went toward the sound. Just as he turned, an arrow sped close by him and vanished into a clump of bushes.

He fell forward and began to crawl rapidly in the direction from which the arrow had come. Out of the grass emerged a slender, dark-haired man, of middle height and middle years, carrying a bow and wearing a tunic that came to his knees. Perscors lay still as the man stalked by, and then leaped up at him, only to grasp nothingness. By the sudden disappearance, Perscors recognized the nature of his enemy; he looked around for a bird. A raven perched in the upper branches of a nearby tree.

"Which shaman are you, hiding there as a raven?"

"Aristaeus" came the croaking reply.

"Why try to put an arrow into me?"

"You have frightened everyone away" was the hesitant answer.

"So that is it," Perscors wearily remarked, looking around at the deserted hills. "I have a bad name here, and the Hyperboreans have fled from me."

"You have a bad name everywhere," the raven retorted crossly.

"I suppose I do, by now," Perscors brooded aloud. "But my only quarrel is with the Archons," he added, and directed a question to the raven: "Do you serve Saklas, or some other Archon?"

"I am a Hyperborean," the raven croaked. "We serve only the sun. Saklas made the sun, but not the true sun, beyond."

"We have no quarrel, then. I am only looking for stolen property, and if Saklas has stationed it here, so much the better."

The raven vanished from the tree. Perscors felt little confidence that he had persuaded the shaman, and resolved to look out for further ambushes. But when he turned to his left, he found the dark-haired archer, standing weaponless and staring at him with curiosity but without hostility.

"Abaris sent you across, yet you are no shaman."

Perscors pondered the statement before he answered: "I dreamed the initiations, but I refused them. They were mixed up with Saklas, Achamoth, and this world of bondage."

"You dreamed the wrong dreams," Aristaeus said. "Those are your own dreams, and not those Abaris would have sent."

"In any case, I am here. Send for your people."

Aristaeus smiled savagely. "They will return after you have marched still farther north. Only Abaris and I have the knowledge you seek."

Perscors shook his head in wonderment, and then found himself laughing out his questions: "Here is a whole planet of Knowers, where no one knows well enough not to provoke me! I came here from a tower, and the twin tower is nearby; but where? Yet I myself don't know precisely what I expect of that tower. What is in it? Why did Saklas steal it from Olam? And why did he move it here?"

Aristaeus appeared bewildered. His reply came in a voice very different from either his raven or human tones. Remote and cold, an ancient voice spoke through him, even as he fell on his back to the ground in front of Perscors and writhed in an ecstatic trance.

"Go farther north until you find a high ladder in a grove of olive trees. Mount it if you dare. What you will see you will see from atop that ladder."

Abandoning Aristaeus where he had fallen, Perscors marched northward through the hills again. When night came, he rested in a broad valley, eating apples from a lovely orchard. He lay down to sleep, and dreamed of the grotesque old Abaris, who had wounded him with a golden arrow.

In the dream, Perscors rode the arrow, now grown to a great size. He moved through space, too high to see earth or Lucifer, until he found himself unexpectedly in a courtyard, an open place, surrounded by low walls, where an audience had gathered around the naked Abaris. Abaris stared at a door at the end of the court-yard, and it seemed to Perscors that the crowd of hunters and herdsmen were careful not to look at the door or to go near it. In his left hand, Abaris held a stick, one end of which had a figurine upon it. The shaman's right hand held two arrows, points upward; the point of each arrow had a bell attached to it. Intoning a wordless song, Abaris accompanied himself by striking the two belled arrows against the stick. As Abaris reached a point of paroxysm in his chant, the audience began to sing wordlessly in chorus.

The augmented sound woke Perscors. Since it continued, he was slow to realize that he was out of the dream. He rose and moved through the dark grove to the other side of the valley, where he beheld the courtyard of which he had been dreaming. Abaris went through the door, the singing ceased, and the Hyperboreans waited in silence as Perscors came up to join them.

CHAPTER **38**

Séance of Abaris

THE HYPERBOREANS fell back as Perscors drew near. Noting that they were unarmed, he walked between them, looking straight ahead as he followed Abaris through the door of a high stone house.

Abaris, ignoring the interruption, continued to stare at a fierce fire on the hearth. After a while, he began to shake violently.

The fire in the hearth burned down. Abaris fell to the floor and lay on his back with his face turned to the south. Piercing cries came first from one direction in the room, then another; cries of lapwing, falcon, and woodcock. Perscors realized that the bird cries were being projected by the shaman.

When silence followed, Abaris rose to a sitting position and began to beat on a small hand drum, while chanting a wordless song. Gradually the song and drumming rose in volume until Abaris was bellowing. Bird calls echoed within the song, and then silence came again abruptly.

A rush of wind heralded the arrival of the shaman's tutelary spirit. The wind, violent and sudden, toppled Abaris over backward. As the fire on the hearth died, then rekindled itself, Abaris leaped upward, drumming continuously. Perscors judged the roof to be ten or eleven feet high, and was startled as the shaman's leaps took him higher and higher, until he scraped the stone ceiling. At his last descent, Abaris cried out fiercely, and then fell forward upon his face.

Perscors went up to the old shaman and turned him over. The face of Abaris was set in trance-like ecstasy. Perscors sat down on the stone floor and waited for the tutelary spirit to speak to him, through his rigid mouth. The voice of Achamoth, mocking and harsh, rose out of the shaman.

"Climb the tree-ladder in the olive grove, even as this fool would have told you. But when you mount into the tower, find me there, and through me your death."

Perscors turned, went out the door, marched past the waiting Hyperboreans out into the valley, and headed north. After so many false starts, he sensed that only now was he at the true beginning of his quest. The menace of Achamoth he ignored wholly.

At dawn, after walking all night, he rested in an olive grove, after determining that there was no shamanistic tree-ladder there. He had willed not to sleep again until he came to Olam's tower, but sleep overcame him. He dreamed that his own tutelary spirit came to him. She appeared as a slight, birdlike woman, unlike any other he had seen, darker than Ruha and draped in blackest silk. She gestured toward an archway, and he went through, only to find her gone and to stand upon another threshold. Archway after archway, and threshold after threshold; he moved on, and at last he emerged onto a half-lit high place, with a great silver ladder hanging in the air, shining before him.

Perscors counted the intricately turned rungs, but when he got to seven, the ladder vanished.

He looked around the high place again and saw that it was a vast landing in a maze of narrowing staircases.

The labyrinth was not roofed everywhere. Perscors walked up one staircase that was lit as if with daylight from above. He moved to another wide landing and found other staircases leading downward.

At one landing he found himself to be standing on a sort of summit. To the right, a wide prospect opened across hilly groves and sudden valleys. In a central grove a high tree-ladder appeared, seven-runged. Then, beyond this, he saw men standing on other summits; they now seemed to be everywhere, and he concentrated his gaze upon one dressed like himself, in Scythian gray. The man slowly toppled down; he had evidently yielded to a vertigo which started to spread, as other men fell from other summits into the same depths. With the vertigo seizing him, Perscors woke up.

It was full day. A few groves ahead, Perscors now knew, he would come to his own tree-ladder, from which the lost tower could be surveyed. Confident of victory, and with the image of fire before him, he took up his march again.

CHAPTER 39

Olam on Origins and Aims

CLOSE BEHIND Perscors, Valentinus and Olam rested in a grassy dell by a waterfall, having marched through the night and the morning. Olam amused himself by throwing stones at the waterfall, while Valentinus, motionless, continued to struggle with returning memories.

He recalled that, in an earlier life, he had journeyed from Alexandria to Rome, in order to clarify his beliefs. Rome he could not remember at all, but an image from the journey crowded upon him. At sunset, on an island just off an Italian port, he had seen a windowless, deformed, and dreary fortress-like building, with a ruined, open tower at its top. In the radiance, the tower's bell had tolled hoarsely, reminding him of a catastrophic experience in a town near Alexandria. What was that experience?

"Pause a moment, Olam, in your stone-throwing labors and help me to remember one thing."

Olam picked up more stones, while grimacing. "No, that is just what I cannot do. You, of all beings, must remember for yourself."

He let the stones drop, and rose. His ugly yellow face was creased with perplexity as he motioned to Valentinus to join him in resuming the journey. Hesitantly, thinking aloud, he began to justify his own reticence: "The origin of every darkness, and of every breaking, is within the Light itself. The tragedy is of the Pleroma. These stones I throw themselves derive from our error and our failure."

Valentinus nodded as he rose. "This rocky world is a battered affection of the Pleroma. When the inwardness fell away from itself, through the passion of Achamoth, this became its furthest reach, outward and downward."

"This abides through ignorance," Olam rejoined, "but the ignorance is only our knowledge reversed. This materiality will pass."

Valentinus, who heard his own doctrine, remained troubled. "But if the godhead is broken, my knowing ought to have helped mend it. On Lucifer as on earth, the knowing seems not to change the known, and yet it should."

Olam answered, but with reluctance: "The knowing makes for change, but very slowly. Have you forgotten why you left Rome?"

"No, but the memory comes slowly. I saw that the Gnosis alone was sufficient for salvation and freedom, and I cast out the sacraments and rituals of the Great Church's mysteries."

As he spoke, there came flooding back over his feelings a part of his old greatness. In vision, he stood in the Roman Church, dividing his auditors forever into those who believed and his own, who knew. Across eighteen hundred years, the power that had surged through the climax of his sermon returned to him, and he said, almost chanting now:

"It is not for us to perform the mystery of divine power through corporeal things wrought by the demiurgic creation. Perfect salvation is the very cognition itself of the ineffable greatness: for since through ignorance came about Defect and Passion, the whole system springing from the Ignorance is dissolved by the Gnosis. Therefore the Gnosis is salvation of the inner man; and it is not corporeal, for the body is corruptible; nor is it psychical, for even the soul is a product of Defect and is as a lodging to the spirit or pneuma; pneumatic, therefore, must be the form of salvation. Through knowledge, then, the inner man, the pneuma is saved; so that to us the knowledge of original being suffices; this is our freedom; this is the true salvation."

Olam listened in great peace, and then waited. But the restoration of his own true voice was only another confusion for Valentinus. He brooded: the clouded image of a tower rose again. On the south of Alexandria, situated above the Mareotic Lake, on a low-lying hill, he had lived for a while in the community of the Therapeutae. The simple, low houses of the society went along the lake to a point where it debouched into the open sea close by. The tower had stood on a high point directly where the sea began. There he had gone, after being driven from Rome.

The Therapeutae had knowledge, but still lived under the old law. Yet they had taken him in, to rest and contemplate. In the tower, at midnight on the seventh Sabbath of his stay, the darkness had come upon him. Achamoth, the Dark Intention who dwelt among the Aeons, had appeared to him that he might be afflicted.

The vision faded away again. Valentinus looked hard at Olam, who was impatient to depart.

"Aeon, if the error and the failure belong to the truth itself, then what is divine is degraded. How will going back to the origin restore me, or even you?"

Olam would not answer. Valentinus went on, but speaking now more to himself. "Or, is this the measure of our strength? That we admit to ourselves, and without perishing, that the world of original being had ceased to be true?"

Olam, provoked to a reply, seized a stone and threw it, underhand but with amazing force, far into the sky. It did not descend. He grinned cheerfully and spoke with assurance: "You are a stone of wisdom, and I sling them. We are both star-destroyers! You threw yourself so high, when first you found me! But every thrown stone—must fall! The aim is not to return to the Pleroma as it was, at the origin! For that All was less than All, that Fullness proved only an emptiness. The aim must be to gain a past from which we might spring, rather than that from which we seemed to derive."

Swiftly they marched together across the fields and groves of the Hyperboreans. Olam, now the more divided of the two, discovered to his chagrin that he had to hasten to keep up.

CHAPTER 40

Place of the Demiurge

PERSCORS MOUNTED the tree-ladder until he stood on the seventh rung. Beyond the next grove was a broken wall set upon a hill, and beyond the hill a lake. At the northern end of the lake, a single tower rose beside the water, set against a cypress grove.

He descended the ladder, and marched through and beyond the next grove, until he had climbed the hill and stood before the broken wall.

It rose above him in fourteen jagged rows of huge stone blocks, facing west. He looked beyond it down to the lake, and north along the lake until he could study the tower. But, to his own surprise, he paused at the wall, troubled by its familiarity.

Where had he seen such mammoth blocks? Phoenician or Roman, the shaped stones carried about them the aura of a temple overthrown.

Perscors shook the impression away, turned north, and descended the hill. As he walked along the lake, shadowed by cypresses, he stumbled upon a rock. Its dimensions startled him. Was it a natural altar, or an exposure of an ordeal to come? Extending from where he stood for some forty feet or so, and curiously symmetrical, as broad as it was long, the rock's evident solidity and strength were greatly impressive to him.

At the rock's midpoint, Perscors knelt to examine what seemed a cistern. Had it been hewn, or was it natural? How deep did it go? Was it a place prepared by Saklas for his prisoners?

Again he shook away forebodings, and marched off the rock toward the tower.

His first impression, as he came closer, was that the tower itself was part of a ruin, a fragment of something that had been larger or more complete. Had it been a gate tower? There was space enough, there at the head of the lake, but he could see no traces of anything lost or destroyed in the large cleared area around the tower.

"It is because of what one has not found," he murmured, as he came close to the square, high tower— stone, backed on a cypress grove, and overlooking what seemed hot sand toward the calm blue water of the lake. It did not resemble the tower on Krag Island, from which he had departed with Olam and Valentinus. Belatedly he realized that he had hoped for a counterpart of that tower.

"Nothing is given back," he said aloud, and then wondered what he meant. He gave up wondering, in need of action.

When he saw that this tower had a door, and that it stood open, he lost himself in a frenzy of laughter.

"Is it so easy then, Saklas? Very well, indeed! May I not be more difficult for you than you expect?"

Perscors went through the open door, to find himself alone in what was unexpectedly a wide, long, low court-yard of a room, bare of any image or furniture. Looking up, he saw only stone and no staircase. At the far end of the room was the source of light, coming through the wide opening of a vestibule. Beyond the opening, Perscors could see a dais, leading to what seemed a closed cedar cube, a small chamber or chapel.

As he entered this holy-of-holies, he felt only indifference, neither curiosity nor dread.

"As empty here as the rest of this place," he said, but then looked up. Directly over his head, the stones opened to disclose a circular brass staircase, winding upward into bright cloud or mist.

"Inside or outside?" he asked softly as he pulled himself onto the stairs. Though he knew he was referring to the mist, he was troubled at his own words.

Rounding the first turn of the stairs, he suddenly confronted a sheet of fire and recoiled from it involuntarily. In the recoil he fell over sideways, and found himself falling outward, as though he were not in the tower.

He came down calmly, in darkness, but on his feet, unhurt yet still startled. Surprise gave way to fury as he realized he stood in mire.

"The cistern," he whispered angrily, pushing his way through bog and darkness. Had it been a cave or even a tomb, he would have lateral access, but how was even he to extricate himself from this floor of excrement?

Perscors heard a roaring as of waters coming in, and

understood that he faced drowning again, with circumstances now more fully in Saklas's control.

Braced against the flood, stunned by the force and tumult as it washed over him, Perscors lost consciousness for some seconds. He revived as he was rushed along, and noticed a huge black rock looming above and ahead of him. With all his will, he fought the waters, and entered a basin-like aperture in the rock. Gasping, he was washed upward and emerged at the mouth of the cistern. The last strength of his anger pulled him up, until he lay drenched at the rock's midpoint. Ahead of him, mocking at his exhaustion and at the defeat of his first attempt, the tower rose at the lake's head. Perscors as yet had no strength to speak, but the words formed in him soundlessly as he glared at the tower:

"I will not go from this place of the Demiurge, until either he or I am consumed in the fire."

CHAPTER **41**

The Dark Intention

A C H A M O T H   S C O W L E D down upon Perscors, who grinned savagely back up at her from the surface of the rock and scrambled to his feet, prepared for a death grapple if need be. She shook her head, with an expression of distaste for his bog-stained body. As she turned away from him, a single disdainful gesture indicated that he was to follow.

Perscors hesitated as he watched her walk south along the lake. Northward lay the fire and Saklas, whose mother was now seeking to defer the end. A frenzy of desire for her, mingled with hatred, fought in Perscors with his own weariness of the quest, with his need to make an end of it, any end. Desire, the deeper need to lacerate the woman, to annihilate her disdain, won in

198

Perscors, to his chagrin. Strength, which had enabled him to refuse Ruha and to evade Nekbael, seemed wholly lacking in him. Lack, he dully sensed, was his center as he followed Achamoth. He felt humiliated that he had no impulse to turn around and attempt the tower again.

"The Mother of God," he whispered bitterly as he followed her, limping somewhat, moved again to anguish and desire by Achamoth's swift, stately movement. She did not deign to look around, but led him quickly south along the lake's sandy shore.

Within one of the cypress groves, she entered a round stone house. He followed warily, looking about lest her handmaidens be poised for an attack; yet this time he seemed alone with her. "Wisdom the Whore," an ancient voice whispered within him, but he was wary now of all voices, whatever their origin.

After he had washed in a great round basin and robed himself in a thick gown, he sat near her before a low table on the fur-covered stone floor. She would not watch him as he ate and drank. He scarcely noted what fruits he devoured with his bread, or when he drank wine or water. Sometimes he stared at her, coldly admiring the contrast between the dark of her hair and the terrible whiteness of her skin. At other moments he saw nothing, but brooded upon the broken wall, the bare holy-of-holies, the cistern, and the ceiling of fire at the first level of the tower stairs.

"I have survived prison, cistern and pitfall, torrent and sea, the desert and night of the Kenoma. What demons are left for me upon Lucifer, except you and your son?"

His tone had been quizzical, since he sat as her guest. Achamoth condescended only to stare at him. The expressionless gaze reminded Perscors of Ruha, and he grew sad.

"You are the demon set loose upon us here. Olam knew you for what you were and are, and brought you here for the combat."

Her voice, even and flat, almost toneless, indicated to Perscors that the final struggle between them was yet to be. Rest before battle, he thought, but then felt a desperate desire for knowledge.

"What was I?"

"He who is born of the mother is brought forth into death and the cosmos, from the dark light to the dark light. So my children were born. But you, and I, were not born of the mother."

Perscors brooded on the words, but without shock. What he had begun to learn among the Manichees, he now began to *know*. The Fall truly had been of the divinity, and not of men and women alone. At the origin of fate came a double divine fall of those not born of the mother, of the Primal Man and the female Thought of God.

"As well myself as another!" He laughed, but this moved her to a sudden bitterness.

"Anguish and terror are beyond your depth! You cannot know an inward suffering, because always you remain a child, though truly you never were the child of anyone! Go on in blindness, die here still blind. It cannot matter. You will wake to life in yet another cosmos, remembering nothing, learning nothing. Abandoned in the void, you will blunder on to another void!"

"Slow!" he whispered back to her hoarsely. "Be just a little slower in having me go to death in this world! I intend to take one or two more with me out of here, whether they waken elsewhere or not."

"You do not make the truth," she answered with a curiously soft decisiveness. "There are negatives in the truth, losses that even such as you must take. You are not here for your own victory, even if you should win. Olam gains, whether you live or die. If you live, you remain his weapon. If you die, then the death purchases full remembrance for Valentinus."

Perscors battled his anger, seeing that madness would take him by it. He knew again that he was not ready to understand her words.

In the long silence ensuing, night came on. Achamoth withdrew to another chamber, but the desire to follow her left him for a while. He had to reflect and to rest, and to sleep if he could, one final night.

He lay down, knowing that tonight, at least, she would not attack him. What had Valentinus said her name meant, when first it had come to him on the cliffs of Krag Island? A dark intention? What was his own purpose, in the time remaining to him? And was it his own?

"Are we not all versions or remnants of Primal Man or of the Thought of God?" He heard his own voice and something too tentative or too exhausted in that voice moved him to a sleepy anger. With the anger came the pride of self-identity, of having discovered his own share in the godhead. And after the pride came the guilt, from the text taught him in childhood:

"Because thy heart is lifted up, and thou hast said: I am a god, I sit in the seat of God, in the heart of the seas;

"Yet thou art man, and not God . . ."

He had chanted loud enough for Achamoth to have heard him, or to have been awakened, if she slept. Drowsy as he was, he would have gone on chanting, yet could not remember more. But just before he fell asleep, another fragment returned, and he recited it softly:

"They shall bring thee down to the pit; and thou shalt die the deaths of them that are slain, in the heart of the seas.

"Wilt thou yet say before him that slayeth thee: I am God?"

"I shall die soon, but I shall not be slain," he whispered fiercely, even as he fell asleep.

In his dream, Perscors returned to the empty cedar chamber of Saklas, only to find two crouching female figures facing each other there. Were they of flesh or of ivory? He saw them in profile: Achamoth and Ruha, or their representations. Each stretched forth both her arms to the other, and behind each arm was a wing.

They crouched upright, their legs bent under so that their knees reached forward to each other and their buttocks rested upon their upturned heels. Arms and legs were naked, but they wore wide metallic collars around their shoulders, and heavy breastplates hung down from their necks. With bare heads and streaming hair, they reached toward but could not touch a small winged cherub set between them.

Perscors stared more intently. Ivory or flesh, the small cherub was a shrunken version of himself. He came up in terror from the dream, and the remainder of the text came back to him:

"Thus saith the Lord God: Thou seal most accurate, full of wisdom, and perfect in beauty, thou hast been in Eden the garden of God; every precious stone was thy covering, the carnelian, the topaz, and the emerald, the beryl, the onyx, and the jasper, the sapphire, the carbuncle, and the smaragd, and gold; the workmanship of thy settings and of thy sockets was in thee, in the day that thou wast created they were prepared. Thou wast the far-Covering Cherub, and I set thee so that thou wast upon the Holy Mountain of God. Thou hast walked up and down in the midst of the stones of the fire . . . But they filled the midst of thee with violence, and thou hast sinned. Therefore I will destroy thee O Covering Cherub, from the midst of the stones of the fire . . . I will bring forth a fire from the midst of thee, it will devour thee, and I will turn thee to ashes . . . thou art become a terror, and thou shalt never be any more."

Perscors had recited this curse in a clear, strong tone, and had listened carefully. Achamoth stood before him, watching intently, her expression alert but poised in some reserve.

He stood up to face her, and he spoke with a bitterness that surprised them both: "They taught me that thus saith the Lord God. But I see now that thus saith the Lord Saklas. Wherever I was, there is no workmanship in me. I am no part of this creation, or of any other. I was one with the Abyss, from whom Saklas stole to make his worlds."

She watched him silently, as though she expected an attack. But he had bathed, eaten, and slept as her guest, and he went forth in her robe. They would meet again as enemies, perhaps to the death. Perscors saluted her gravely, and went out into the night.

CHAPTER **42**

Aeon and Archon

THAT NIGHT, Olam and Valentinus had gone separate ways, agreeing to meet at midnight later, when they
would depart from Lucifer. Valentinus marched around
the western edge of the lake, while Olam followed the
eastern path to the tower, at the lake's northern edge.

Olam grunted as he went by the huge stone wall, and
he spared a single snort for the black rock.

"Saklas's toys," he muttered, and went on up to the
tower.

But on arriving there, he became uneasy, and did not
enter.

"Too quiet," he mumbled again, and sat down upon a
single slab of loose stone, some distance back from the

iron door. Wherever Perscors was, he was not in the tower.

"If the mad giant indeed had been caught in some trap, he is out of it again by now. He is most likely playing love-and-death games with Achamoth! Someone will be murdered, anyway!"

After cheerfully reviewing the possibilities aloud. Olam composed himself for some contemplation. He felt pleased enough with himself. Perhaps Saklas had been a touch cleverer than usual, but it had gone well enough. At least everyone had converged upon the right place! Valentinus was being a little recalcitrant and solitary, but then he had been something of a problem long before. Perscors was rather wild even as embodiments of the Primal Man went, but he was certainly not Olam's responsibility. Doubtless he would maim or destroy another Archon or two and perhaps rid this particular cosmos of a few vicious presences.

"Minor gains, side benefits!" Olam chuckled. As good humor grew in him, he leaped over contemplation and happily fell asleep.

But he failed to dream his customary dreams. The visions that held together the living book of his eternal life as an Aeon avoided him. He writhed on the stone slab, indignantly dreaming another life, one which he could not recognize at all. Achamoth was in the arms of the life he dreamed, and that personification was violently penetrating the demoness, in a jagged, disordered rhythm of deep thrusts, long pauses, and hurried, twisted soundings of her depths and shallows. No music of their motions claimed any part of their coupling as tenderness. Trapped in the dream, Olam furiously tried to disengage from the dream's actor, but the more fierce his effort, the more tightly he embraced Achamoth. Her eyes shone with a dark light of laughter as Olam intensified their mutual imprisonment of body in body. With an effort that blacked out something vital in him, Olam finally smashed himself awake, to find himself bruising his own head repeatedly upon a ridge in the slab of stone.

He was badly hurt, he realized, as he pulled himself up and staggered into a cypress grove. Despite the pain's intensity and his own anxiety at the extent of physical self-damage, his greatest suffering was shame that he could have been so vulnerable to sorcery.

"Take on materiality, and take on ignorance," he groaned out as he doubled up against the trunk of a cypress tree. The tree gave against his weight, tottered, and, with almost a moan, was uprooted abruptly; he fell over hard with it. He scrambled up blindly, fighting for self-control, as he began to know the danger of the contest. The true ownership of the tower might be his, but he had journeyed in a material guise into a world otherwise wholly the Demiurge's, and he had let himself be trapped in a moment of unwariness.

A titanic storm burst from the night around him, and the entire grove cracked, gasped, and came crashing down, spitting smoke. Hunched over, shielding his head, Olam ran to the lake's edge and dived in. Swimming with terrible velocity, he bounded out of the water and into the tower's open entrance. Once inside, he rested on the stone floor, watching the lightning and torrents of the Demiurge descend outside, but knowing that the tower was not subject to the world of the storm god, for truly it was not Saklas's.

CHAPTER 43

A Ruined Shrine

SEEKING REFUGE from the sudden storm, Perscors darted into one of the cypress groves, where he
dodged the crashing and smoldering trees. Running farther east, he took shelter just beyond the grove, within
massive stone ruins in a circular clearing, on high
ground. Because of the night and the torrent, he could
make out only the roughest shape of the ruined structure,
and then only by the intermittent lightning.

When the storm ended as abruptly as it had begun,
Perscors felt himself to be upon the threshold of some
great change. A moonlit night had succeeded the storm,
and by what he knew to be the light of Achamoth he
investigated the ruined shrine of his refuge.

The stone building he stood in seemed to have had

holes torn in all its sides and its roof, as though the masonry were cloth. It was a longhouse, quite empty, and all one continuous room. He recalled having seen houses somewhat like this on a tour of Palestine. A search revealed nothing minute or hidden.

Outside it, in the moonlit compound, Perscors counted six other ruined houses, each with gaps ripped into stone sides and roofs. He did not bother to enter any, anticipating that all were similarly empty.

At the center of the clearing, what may have been an altar rose from a black rock. So uneven were its pieces that Perscors could not decide if something had been deliberately overthrown there or whether some random violence had scattered its stones.

Just off to the left of the rock there was a glinting in the moonlight. He walked to it, reached down, and retrieved an ivory figurine, some eighteen inches in height; it was surprisingly heavy. When he held it up in full moonlight, he saw that it was a miniature Perscors, winged and armed with lance and dagger. Its eyes, sapphires set deep in the ivory, glared at him as he raised this cherub to the sky.

Then he set it down. Was this, then, a sanctuary where he himself had been worshipped? And if there had been a cult of Primal Man upon Lucifer, who had destroyed it, Saklas or Achamoth?

What had happened to his followers? Their sanctuary destroyed, had they been exiled or murdered?

He stood in the moonlight, lamenting only what he felt to be his lost glory. After a few moments he became aware of another light. He set aside the robe of Achamoth and stood in the cold night wind. A strong heat began to emanate both within and out from him. Around him in the cleared space the light condensed into concentric circles. Circle upon circle they extended and the farthest was a deep blue. He realized that this blue rim was the periphery of the pupils of his own eyes.

"My epiphany is here!" he shouted ecstatically into the winds, which rose to a sudden force, almost to a gale, yet failed to drown out his cry.

The desire to find Valentinus was now dead in him. He began to believe that he belonged neither to the Aeons, with their alien god of the Abyss, nor to the Archons, bound to their own creation.

"I am prior to all of these," he whispered into the wind.

Knowledge was not the goal of his quest. He would go up to the tower to destroy Saklas and Achamoth, but not because they blocked him from access to the truth. They were usurpers who had stolen his sovereignty and dimmed his glory. He would avenge this wrong, but what would come after his revenge he could not yet know. Resolutely, and therefore untroubled by ultimates, he turned back toward the tower to accomplish not a task his fate might have assigned him but that very fate itself.

CHAPTER **44**

The Way In and Up

A T   T H E northeast corner of the lake, Valentinus stood in front of another tower. It was situated above the lake on a low-lying hill, rocked by continuous winds both from the lake and from what Valentinus now could observe as an open sea into which the lake debouched.

"The tower of the Therapeutae, above the Mareotic Lake of Alexandria; yet I am here alone."

As he spoke, memories returned to him. He had sought out the Therapeutae because those monastics of the old law knew enough to worship the Self-existent who is better than the Good, purer than the One, and more primordial than the Creator, whom their fathers had worshipped.

For seven weeks he had been their guest. Every seventh day he had attended their assembly, when they met together and sat in order according to their age in the proper attitude, with their hands inside their robe, the right hand between the breast and the chin and the left withdrawn along the flank.

After seven weeks had passed, they assembled for his discourse. White-robed and with faces in which cheerfulness was combined with the utmost seriousness, they took their stand in order, their eyes and hands lifted up to the Self-existent, and they prayed that their feasting might be acceptable.

"How clearly the scene returns!" Valentinus called out joyously. Their seats, when they reclined, were plank beds of the common kinds of wood, raised slightly at the arms to give something to lean on. No wine was brought, but only the brightest and clearest water. The table was kept pure from the flesh of animals; the food laid on it was loaves of bread, with salt as seasoning. Tears came to Valentinus's grim face as he remembered the flavor of hyssop, which had permeated the holy bread.

To these people, the whole book of the laws was a living creature, with the literal ordinances for its body, and for its soul the invisible mind laid up in its wording. There came back to him now something close to the end of the discourse that he had given them on the eve of the fiftieth day:

"Each one will speak concerning the place from which he has come forth, and to the region from which he received his essential being, he will hasten to return once again . . ."

The memory departed, even as Valentinus listened intently to his own voice. He needed to hear more, but he remembered no more to speak.

He had kept walking, and was at the open entrance of the tower.

"Is this truly the tower of the Therapeutae, or is it of the Sophia-Prunikos, Wisdom the Whore, who fell into Achamoth?"

He asked the question aloud, and a male voice whispered out of the wind, close to his left ear: "Enter, for the way is in and up. I entered the vileness of Tyre and redeemed the latest and lowest fallen Thought of God. Shall you do less?"

Valentinus hesitated, until the voice became more urgent: "In every heaven I took on a different form, according to the form of the beings in each heaven, that I might remain concealed from the Archons and descend to the Sophia, who is called also Prunikos and Holy Spirit, through whom I created the angels, who then created the world and man."

Revulsion overcame Valentinus upon the threshold. He remembered now the voice of Simon Magus of Samaria, who deemed himself the Favored One, and shouted against the charlatan's voice: "I did not come for spurious miracles or as a sham of the godhead! Nor did I come to hear your false claims once more. And it is not for me to raise up a fallen Wisdom . . ."

But his own voice trailed off, as the driven-down memories rose up again. He had departed from the Therapeutae just past midnight, as the day turned into his fiftieth with them. Achamoth, or his own weakness at confronting her, had thrust him out of the tower and into the bewilderment of the Kenoma.

Valentinus swayed with nausea and self-contempt,

until he fell across the threshold. He was aware of a woman's laughter and dragged himself up to stand unsteadily just within the tower, looking up at the night sky. After a few moments, he understood that the stars were laughing at him.

CHAPTER 45

Perscors Archon

As again he came up to the northwest tower, Perscors stopped in surprise at seeing Olam limp past him. The Aeon's yellow face scowled in pain as he stumbled into the grove, looking straight ahead and failing to see Perscors.

"It has been too much for old Olam!" declared Perscors. "Here, in my world, usurped by the Archons, the Knowers have no fire of their own to battle the storms of Saklas! But what fresh goblin is this?"

Perscors moved from laughter to amused contempt as another being, unknown to him, advanced from the grove and stood, armed but irresolute, in front of the tower's entrance. Less than six feet tall, and slight in frame, he would have represented no menace, except

that he was in full armor, with shield and sword,
whereas Perscors was naked and unarmed, except for the
blue circle of light stretching seven feet about him.

"Speak, hobgoblin! Better that I learn something
about you before I hurl you into the grove!"

There was a strong contrast between the blazing
armor of the being that Perscors taunted and the pale-
ness of the face, at once sullen and baffled, far more
amazed by Perscors than Perscors could be by anyone.
The armor was afire with carnelian, topaz, emerald,
diamond, beryl, onyx, jasper, sapphire, and carbuncle,
all set in purest gold. A second glance made plain to
Perscors that the armor was outsized for his antagonist,
and that the emerald-studded shield and sword were also
too large and were brandished very awkwardly.

"Speak out, and say something for yourself!" Perscors
roared again. "And whose stolen finery are you wearing?"

The realization came to Perscors, without reservation,
that this was his own armor and his own sword. In fury,
he charged at his silent enemy, evading the sword that
flashed by him and knocking the shield away. Perscors's
impetus was so great that he landed on the ground,
stretched atop an unconscious foe.

"Short work!" he growled, and rose to his knees, rapidly stripping the armor off. Only after he had assumed
the armor himself, and held both shield and sword, did
he deign to glance again at his victim, who lay now gasping in the moonlight. A strange glitter rose from the
naked and trembling body, whose bruises were palpable.

"Wretched thief, come forth with a few words or I'll
hack you up a bit with this sword that you usurped!"

Faltering at first, but then in a steady monotone, another story of the origins emerged:

"I am Helel, the Cosmocrator. It was my right to defend my tower against you, here in the utmost North. My star defies sunrise, at the end of each night. Here, beyond the north wind, my word would be law, were it not for Saklas, whose storms rule me also. But this is my world, upon which you are the wanderer and the alien. On this world, the cherub's armor always has been mine. Whose it has been elsewhere, I cannot say. I am Helel Archon, also called Lucifer, son of the dawn and lord of the Tower of Assembly. But who can stand against an otherworldly demon? Let your quarrel now be against Saklas and Achamoth, and may they have the strength to destroy you! But I am overthrown, and out of the battle, made weak by my own knowing . . ."

Perscors tried to puzzle it out, but though his anger waned, he understood only a little.

"The armor, anyway, precisely fits me and not you! A puny world this is indeed, with you as its guardian! But what do you know that Saklas can't know? Are you not his creature?"

The effort of speech had exhausted the badly bruised Helel, who whispered forth the rest of his story: "The Demiurge Saklas is a creature of his mother Achamoth, but from the psychical substance and not from the spirit. I am the Demiurge's creature, but from the spiritual substance, from the grief and perplexity of the mother, and so of the pneuma. I *know* the Abyss, but Saklas cannot know. You are stronger than the Aeon who inflicted you upon us . . ."

"You leave me no wiser," Perscors grunted. "But it doesn't matter anyway. Poor little devil that you are, crawl into the cypresses and lick your wounds there."

In contempt and some wonderment, Perscors turned

away from the fallen Helel and back toward the tower. Proper foes were what he needed, he thought, and a truer combat might resolve some puzzlements. Shield and sword at the ready, brave in his own armor, he entered the tower.

Achamoth stood before him, just past the threshold. Scorn marked her countenance as she surveyed him.

"Perscors Archon, prepared to do slaughter! Welcome then! But what if there is no ogre here but you to slay? What if we have no violence suitable for you? You, who were too early for us, may find that we are too late in the story to have any resistance left against you. Welcome again! Be my guest yet once more ere this night is over."

Foolish and forlorn, he waited upon the threshold. In the face of Achamoth, he was a child again, unarmed for the subtle combat, overarmed for the battle he could not find.

CHAPTER **46**

Bewilderment

P E R S C O R S S A T on the bare floor of the tower. The shield and sword were by his side. He looked down at the gold and precious stones of his armor. Had he recovered his identity so uselessly? Yet the perfect fit of the armor remained an obscure comfort to him. Perhaps, he reflected, it was a sign that his coming fate would fit him also.

Opposite him, Achamoth sat as though she were daydreaming. Her expression was blank, and she looked through him.

He had to pause, he decided. If above he were to find only the fire and then an emptiness, then this tower did not hold his fate. If he showed patience enough, Achamoth might lead him to Saklas or otherwise instruct him for the final combat.

It was a relief, he realized now, that there would be only words between them. No lovemaking and no violence; the impulses that had driven him toward her had left him. Their fates were separate. Darkly he understood something of what she had meant in saying that he was both too early and too late for her story.

He studied her face, and thought of Valentinus. If his friend, now forever lost to him, suffered from the absence of memory, then Achamoth's case was just the opposite. The presence of memory was for her a continuous torment.

It came to him also that he would not understand her story, however much of it she chose to tell him. It was a story that Valentinus would understand, he mused.

A heaviness came upon him and he fell asleep as he waited.

In dream he threaded his way through a labyrinth, following a scarlet cord that Achamoth had let down. He went through what seemed a sea beast's mouth, cut in the rock, and emerged into an open, circular, dark space. Around him, ranged on seats, were men in armor like his own watching him silently. Back, beyond the seated questers, a great fire burned on every side.

He came awake, and seized his sword and shield. But Achamoth sat as she had before, except that now she looked at him with curiosity.

"Have I dreamed what is to come, or part of it?"

She did not answer. Was it that he now confused her?

"It is only an hour until dawn," Perscors said, and an appeal had come into his tone.

"I understand," Achamoth said, adding: "It will be your last morning upon Lucifer."

"Let me conclude by noon, then. Where is Saklas and how am I to get to him?"

"It matters little. He will not fight you, anyway. However you seek him, he will evade you. Try to understand that you are a terror to him."

"Why was I brought here?" Perscors burst out.

"To defeat the Demiurge," she replied coldly. "To so frighten Saklas that he would be distracted from Olam's one aim, which is to restore full memory to Olam's prophet."

Bewilderment mastered Perscors, until he could formulate a last question, painfully: "Why cannot Saklas try to destroy Valentinus?"

"Because your strange friend has been with the dead for eighteen hundred mortal years. Even the Archons cannot slay the dead."

"What remains for me?" Perscors whispered, but the question was directed only to himself.

"I only know what remains for me," she said drily. "I will go to the other tower and tell Valentinus what he needs to be told."

Perscors shook his head bitterly. He no longer desired any understanding, but he would not acknowledge defeat.

"Go where you will. Valentinus will be equal to you, whether he was before or not. But I am here to some purpose still and I shall discover it before I die."

Achamoth rose and went out of the tower, without looking at Perscors again.

Holding his sword and shield, bent over against the

stone floor, he listened hard for the voice that he felt must come.

While he waited, the light began to edge into the tower. He rose and stood in the tower's entrance. Then he went out and turned east along the lake's northern shore, marching defiantly into the sunrise.

CHAPTER **47**

Last Morning on Lucifer

PERSCORS HAD not gone far when the first voice spoke to him, just to his left. He could not tell whether it and the later voices were male or female.

"Why live any longer, alien? Die in your grief, because you cannot get hold of the light. Die the death of air!"

"It is not my light," Perscors answered. "Let Achamoth grieve. I go against every false light."

He was nearly halfway along the northern shore when another voice spoke, this time out of the lake: "Lie down and die near the water, alien! Die in the affection of fear!"

"What should I fear?" Perscors cried. "Let Achamoth fear, lest life like the light would leave her! I am beyond the fear of those that hope, the fear of water!"

As he swung along the shore, he stopped, in a moment of surprise. Ahead of him was a low hill, and on it a second tower.

Before he could resume his march, the third voice whispered to him from the ground he stood upon: "Die the death of earth, Perscors. You are a living death of bewilderment. Lie down and die!"

"I have been bewildered always, long before I came to Lucifer! What I could endure in my own world I can endure here!"

Between Perscors and the tower was a single row of cypresses. As he marched under them, a fourth voice called out from the trees: "Die the death of fire, wanderer! All that you are is the fire of your own ignorance! Lie down beneath the trees and die!"

The row of cypresses burst into flame, and the nearest came crashing down upon Perscors. He fended it off with his shield, and marched past the fire beyond, crying out: "*My* fire, *my* ignorance, *my* dark affection, and so *my* will only, when I choose to die!"

He stood before a dark tower, with its entrance open. After a moment, he shook his head and turned away.

A fifth voice, a voice that was great within him, spoke out, and yet it was not quite his own voice: "Die only the death of the turning back, the soul's own death."

He agreed, but where was the death to be found? Not at either tower, the one empty except for the fire of his own ignorance, nor this one, which was for Achamoth and Valentinus to confront. His fate was elsewhere. He turned into the dawn darkness of the grove and plunged into the shadows.

Some moments later he reached the beginning of his end. The grove receded, and he came to a cleared circle, surrounded by rocks. So many cave entrances beckoned! Was he to search them one by one?

He looked down. The frayed end of a scarlet cord was at his feet. His gaze followed the cord's windings until it vanished into the mouth of what seemed barely a cave.

"More an opening in the stony ground," he said and went up to it.

"Whether this is a trap or not, Saklas, is of little concern to me! With gratitude for the gift, Achamoth!"

Shouting her name, he went down into the world below.

CHAPTER **48**

The Labyrinth

T H E   C A V E   mouth led unaccountably to some rough steps cut in the rock. They descended in a slow turning, and the passageway remained just high enough for Perscors to move through it without stooping. The light from above soon gave out, but as he moved deeper inward and downward, he noticed that a cold reddish glow seemed to illuminate the steps ahead of him. He followed the scarlet cord into a chamber. This wide, twelve-sided space, with twelve corridors opening off it, revealed to him where the light came from. His own armor was glowing, but without heat; the gold and jewels combined to release an intense light.

He went up to one of the corridor openings, and then another and yet another. They all led down into darkness; choosing one, he proceeded down it for a short while until he reached another chamber, one of twelve, like the earlier one but, since uncrossed by the trail of the red cord, clearly as different from the first as it seemed identical to it. Perscors retraced his steps, re-entered the first hall, and tried another of the exits, sensing that the result would be the same. It was, as it was with all the others. Finally he spun himself around, entered a corridor at random, and proceeded hastily and without rational choice from chamber to chamber.

"A labyrinth beyond all others," he angrily brooded aloud, hopelessly lost after an hour's wanderings. This was not a maze of branching alternatives but one in which every choice blossomed in a spray of new uncertainties. The red cord, which Perscors now knew was Achamoth's sign, had soon played itself out, and he was left only with his confusion: he now no longer knew whether he was reentering places he had been before.

"Let it be a snare or trap; I am still ready." But his defiance was lost in animal sounds coming from the next chamber. Perscors rushed ahead to combat with them. As he entered it, he found himself confronted by what he took at first to be four beasts: lion, bull, serpent, and dog. The flickering light given off by his armor revealed them to be men or demons wearing animal masks and squatting horridly. Glad to see them armed with javelins and daggers, rather than more dangerous and invincible weapons, he closed on them, but they fled into four separate corridors; it was impossible to pursue them.

"No one on Lucifer will meet me face to face!" he exclaimed, but then fell silent with the thought that perhaps he had underestimated Saklas, even as Olam had been deceived. The cowardly masked demons were bait, and surely Saklas was fishing for him here in this maze. He remembered a text, and spoke it into the darkness.

"I will spread my net over him and he shall be taken in my snare . . . for the treason he has committed against me."

What they had taught him to be the words of Yahweh, he saw now to be the words of Saklas. If he was in this labyrinth to be netted, then he needed wariness more than his rage for war.

He continued forward, but more cautiously, feeling his way. Without knowing why, he sank suddenly to his knees. The armor light showed nothing untoward ahead, but he reached forward and probed the ground with his sword. The packed clay parted swiftly. Scraping the clay aside, he uncovered what gradually was revealed as a shallow pit lined with spikes arranged in concentric circles, but barely visible even in the light he bore.

Had Achamoth known of this pitfall? He shrugged. This was no way through to Saklas. Any one pit could be evaded, but the traps would be endless. He called aloud: "I have little time left."

The chill words echoed in the labyrinth: "little time left." Perscors rose and pondered his course. His dreams, so far, had not been fit guidance. At best these windings would bring him to Siniavis again, where his shadow self had been defiled and murdered. He could make a great slaughter of the demons there, yet the Demiurge would create them again, under the guidance of Achamoth. If the quest on Lucifer was to end, it must at least conclude in the maiming of the Demiurge. No, the conquest of this labyrinth could itself be a far worse trap than any of those it contained.

He turned resolutely from the place of the pit, catching his spear inadvertently against the side of the cement corridor. It clanged loudly, but the sound died away in the rush of echoing, apparently from the chamber ahead. Perscors followed quickly into it: the echo of the clanging was barely audible, except that, remarkably, it sounded loud and clear in one of the twelve openings. Perscors followed this corridor into another chamber, where he found, again, that the sound of the echo chose only one exit. And so it was by clanging his sword against his shield that he was able to move his way out of the maze, his ear guiding him through confusions that almost maddened the eye.

Perscors finally emerged from the cave into the circle of stones. But his weary wanderings had taken many hours. Looking up, he saw that the sun of Saklas was almost directly overhead. Where was he to discover his adversary?

He turned and brooded on the rocks. No images came to him: their shapes were as adamant even to fancy as they were to touch. The squalor of defeat mounted in Perscors. He lay face down upon a large rock. The will to rise again ebbed from him, and yet he gripped both shield and sword tightly.

Somewhere a faintly rushing noise sounded behind him. Was it water or the movement of fire? He did not care enough to raise his head.

Gradually the sense grew in him that he was being watched. He resisted the feeling, wishing only to be one with the stone upon which he rested.

Somewhere, farther behind him, a horn sounded. A trumpet's call replaced it, in alternation with the cry of yet another trumpet.

Lying upon his face, Perscors listened to the faint exchange between the two trumpets.

"They are singing some god to a battle," he murmured into the rock. But whom could that god battle?

Perscors drowsed off, but only for a few moments. As he came awake, the two trumpets cried out to one another from much closer to him.

He rose sluggishly and turned around. Suddenly it came upon him that this was indeed the place! Mists had enshrouded the noonday sun, but in the semidarkness Perscors detected a light neither from above nor from himself. All about the open, circular, darkened space in which he stood, a horizon of fire burst forth like an imprisoning dawn. Between that distant fire and himself, uncertainly in the midst, Perscors felt rather than saw a wilderness of spectators. Whoever they were, he knew that they came to view the last of him.

He stood ready on the rocky ground.

As the winds blew in upon him, Perscors realized his danger. Saklas indeed was coming to the combat, for the Demiurge had been goaded beyond desperation. But the god would come as wind and cloud.

"I have set myself against the invisible. So let it be. At the least, he and I must grapple."

Barely were the words out when the great winds came in against Perscors.

CHAPTER **49**

End of the Quest

BEHIND PERSCORS, the sound of waters almost convinced him that the lake was crying out in pain. The rocks trembled, and the clouds now flooded forth water, even as the skies sent out a sound of mourning. Did arrows or lightning dart by him? Perscors asked himself. A voice spoke his name in the high wind, or was that the thunder? Drenched and uncertain, but exultant, Perscors stood in the stone circle.

The stones shook and quaked, and smoke rose up all about Perscors. He stood upon burning coals in a darkness, and then he was thrust off his feet as hailstones mixed with boltlike flaming arrows flew all about him. Rolling to his left until he could find solid rock again, Perscors rose, but he had lost shield and sword.

A lightning-arrow struck his left side, yet was deflected by the armor. The force of the blow spun Perscors around, and as he turned he looked up to the sky's northern quarter. The wings of the storm wind darkened the sky, or were those actual wings?

A terrible darkness appeared directly in front of Perscors. Out of the midst of it a huge double ax swung at him and smashed into his left arm. Pain and shock sent Perscors to his knees; the armor had given way and his arm was severed.

Roaring his own name, he charged into the darkness, which receded before him, the double ax being flung aside. A body twisted away from the grasp of his right hand. Raising his right fist, still rushing forward, Perscors put all the strength of his furious will into one blind downward blow. His hand broke at the impact, but his invisible enemy shouted in terrible agony.

Perscors fell upon the fiery stones. A glance ahead showed him the retreating Saklas, dragging his shattered back into the shelter of the cypresses.

The will to follow the maimed Demiurge ebbed in Perscors. He felt neither pain nor desire but only the peace of exhaustion. After a few moments, a fire broke forth from his own loins. When he realized that it was indeed his own fire, he smiled in contentment. Triumph was his final thought as his head became the fire.

CHAPTER 50

Valentinus at the Dark Tower

''F R O M M Y turning back, all the Soul of the world and of the Demiurge took its origin; from my fear and grief, the body of the world and of the Demiurge had its beginning.''

Achamoth stood in the top chamber of the northeastern tower, attempting to instruct Valentinus, who shook his head impatiently, like a man being told what he already knows.

"Seek not to teach me my own speculation. Tell me what only you can know; tell me what you told me once, far back, the telling of which afflicted me and sent me into the silence."

The storm that raged outside the tower suddenly ceased. Achamoth raised her head and frowned bitterly. "There will be no storms to prevent your departure from

Lucifer. The battle is over. Saklas my son is badly wounded and I must go to him."

The urgency of Valentinus's tone detained her. "I have not come to change you, or to hasten the end, but only to remember. You halted my prophecy once. Give back only what you took away then."

She frowned with her own impatience to depart. "My memory too has waned. I know what I was and what I am. But you know my story."

"The story alone, no matter who told it, would not have driven me out to vanish into the desert. You came to me at Pentecost, in the tower of the Therapeutae, and deranged me. The time and the world are different, yet this is that tower!"

She struggled to remember, but nothing came. Smiling a little in farewell, Achamoth turned away to descend the tower. The soft echoes of her final footfalls reverberated in the chamber.

Valentinus climbed the stairway and pulled himself up to the tower's flat roof. Achamoth was already out of sight, vanished into the cypresses. Looking west, he gazed long at the other tower, knowing it to be empty.

Halfway between the towers, he saw Olam, standing rigidly upright by the side of the lake. Something in his stance seemed strange to Valentinus, but he returned to his own broodings. After some moments, lost in himself, he resolved to descend.

But he halted on the stairs, halfway down the tower. A sense of defeat oppressed him, and an actual vertigo made him grip the staircase with both hands. His strength of desperation crumbled chunks of the stone stairs away, and he rolled partway down the steps.

How long he lay prostrate he did not know. Consciousness wavered, but did not leave him. He understood, despite his helplessness, that his predicament could not be the work of the Demiurge, who had been expelled from the struggle. It was the lesser Archons, bereft of their master, who sought to injure him.

Flickeringly at first, but then more steadily, a figure materialized on the landing just below where Valentinus lay. The being grinned up at him. Studying the face, Valentinus realized that it was his own. Speech returned to him, in a shocked whisper.

"Not Achamoth, but you! The *antimimon pneuma*, my Counterfeit Spirit! My psyche feigning the glory of my spark."

His double, now fully materialized, continued to smile triumphantly at Valentinus. Memory and rage flooded back together, and Valentinus painfully scrambled up to confront this mockery of himself.

"You entered my soul and overgrew me, hardened and enclosed me, and made me impotent to know!"

The double, still smiling, bent down to retrieve a jagged chunk of stone that Valentinus had broken away. Straightened up again, the Counterfeit Spirit mounted toward Valentinus, the stone held high over its head by both hands, ready to strike.

"Elaborated error," Valentinus unflinchingly cried. "Dissolve back into the ether!"

The stone fell and crumbled upon the lower stairs. Valentinus peered into the half light, but his double was gone.

"The heart," Valentinus brooded, "is unclean and the abode of many demons. But what could this weak counterfeit have said or done to block me up for so many centuries?"

Musing, he descended the remaining stairs until he came to the tower's open door. But he could not bring himself to go out, the puzzle unsolved. Whether Achamoth had appeared to his double, or a counterfeit Achamoth to his true self, the repressed image or thought that had wounded him would not return. How was he again to proclaim knowledge, he who was ignorant of his own catastrophe?

"A degraded godhead," he said slowly. "And a degraded heresiarch to celebrate it."

He would go to Olam, he decided. The Aeon might know no more than he did, but at least he would know how to continue the struggle.

"I am darker than this tower, as dark as any cave," Valentinus said, and went out into the clear afternoon of a world momentarily free of its maker.

CHAPTER **51**

Olam at the Pleroma

HALFWAY BETWEEN the towers Olam, still stunned, stared at the waters of the lake. The waters rose up and were one with the air.

Olam looked down. Rock and water and air flowed into one another.

He understood then that it was not his wounds that made the vision. The combat must have gone against Saklas, and this world, for now, had opened to the Aeons.

Olam tried to remember when he had last been at the Fullness, but then he saw that he need not remember. The goodness of the Abyss was all around him.

He looked for his brethren.

"But I am here alone."

Where, then, were the others? He had not expected all of the Aeons, for only when all the worlds came to an end, in one act, would all together go into the Pleroma.

But why should he be alone in the Fullness?

That it was the Fullness, he knew beyond knowing. He stood in the pure Abyss, in the Forefather.

He tried to recall to whom he owed this gift, but already he had forgotten the name of that last incarnation of Primal Man. It was not required of him that he should remember.

There was no trouble in him, yet the solitude surprised him.

He walked up to the heights. The stillness was profound, and the pure serenity healed his wounds.

Yet he knew he was but one of thirty. Could so many have strayed or been detained?

Perhaps it did not matter. The Fullness was in him, and he was in the Fullness. He was, at last, in his place of rest.

Why not abide here?

A voice called to him from outside the Pleroma: "Olam!"

He did not answer. Why stir from out of this great peace?

"Olam!"

He drifted away from the call.

But a thought entered to disturb him. Was he the last?

It could not be that the divine degradation had gone that far. And the peace was necessary to him. Other Aeons would be called, and would answer . . .

"Olam!"

The third call moved through him. It was the voice of

Valentinus, a voice that had roused him before and that would not let him rest.

"Here I am," he cried out gruffly, and discovered himself staring at the lake. Valentinus stood by his side, watching him intently.

A terrible pain returned to Olam's head, and with a groan he came out of the peace of the Abyss and back to the worlds of estrangement.

CHAPTER **52**

Freedom

THEY WERE preparing to depart, though only the two of them. Valentinus postponed meditation upon the loss of the third.

Olam, engrossed in the forthcoming flight, had returned to his customary rough cheerfulness. Spells of pain continued to afflict him, but their duration and intensity lessened each hour. By midnight and departure, the Aeon calculated, only traces would remain.

Valentinus stood apart on the hill of the Therapeutae, overlooking the serene ocean. In the calm twilight, memory of his own speculation became complete for him. The ancient cause of his failure of nerve remained hidden, but he had accepted that lapse.

What, then, did he know, he thought to himself, and how could he sum up the knowledge?

He knew freedom.

Between the cosmos, between all of the heavenly systems and spaces, and the true, alien God, our Abyss, there was eternal war.

In that war, a person's self or spark fought on the side of the alien God.

But the sparks have fallen into the cosmos; they sleep in the prison of the cosmos, and do not know how to escape from prison.

The call from the Abyss calls to freedom.

But the battle is endless, and even the spark that has answered the call cannot go home to freedom until all the systems and spaces are destroyed.

Valentinus gazed at the ocean and thought with love of the Therapeutae.

He passed into reverie, and from reverie into his own Pleroma, his own place of rest.

Toward midnight, Olam came for him. It required many efforts for the Aeon to startle Valentinus back to the world.

He returned from the Pleroma slowly and reluctantly, murmuring so softly that Olam could not hear him.

"What were you chanting when I pulled you back?"

"The end of my discourse to the Therapeutae," Valentinus said, his voice softer than it had been before.

"How did it end?" Olam asked.

"Such is the place of the blessed; this is their place," Valentinus answered. "As for the others, then, may they know, in their place, that it does not suit me, after having been in the place of rest, to say anything more."